To G...

Daniel W. Hall

SPARK
OF
MADNESS

Daniel W. Hall

PublishAmerica
Baltimore

Hardcover 978-1-4560-0733-1
Softcover 978-1-4560-0732-4
PUBLISHED BY PUBLISHAMERICA, LLLP
www.publishamerica.com
Baltimore

Printed in the United States of America

Other books by Daniel W. Hall

Frontier Hearts, the story of Captain John Mathias
From Buckskins to Boots, an illustrated book of poems
A Man Named John

Forgiveness is easy,
in theory

1

The casually dressed man with flecks of grey in his hair sat in an uncomfortable chair in an uncomfortable room across from a middle aged man in a prison uniform. He had a pen, a note pad and questions.

"So I guess the first question would have to be, why?"

"Why?" The prisoner laughed and shifted in the chair, making the shackles clink together. "Why? If you had ever felt the soft flesh of a throat in your hands and watched the fear rise to the ultimate pinnacle of human emotion and then watched it fade away with the life that once held it, you wouldn't have to ask." His eyes narrowed. "And don't give me that judgmental look of disgust because it's in all of us. Everyone has it in them to do it."

Interviewer - "Do what?"

"Sin. That's what. To commit the most heinous of crimes known to man. All they need is the right motive and opportunity. They'll do it. I've seen them do it."

Interviewer - "You made them?"

"No, I didn't need to make them do it. I just gave them the motive and the opportunity, that's all."

Interviewer - "You think anybody can commit murder?"

"Think it? I know it." He smirked and sat back. "I had a Sunday school teacher that thought a person could be good." He laughed. "Not just good, but 'perfect and holy,' as he put it, like God. He had a perfect little family and his perfect little wife, and condemned anyone that didn't live up to his standards. So I made phone calls to his house and then hung up when he answered. If she answered, I told her it was the wrong number and that's what she would tell him. I put little crumpled up notes in their car with meaningless dates on them."

He chuckled at the memory of his craftiness. "I could see him fight the thoughts that his perfect little wife was cheating on him. On one hand he knew it couldn't be true, but on the other, he couldn't deny the evidence. I—ha, ha, ha—I even sprayed cologne in the car, on the passenger's seat. You should have seen their perfect little world come apart. He began to preach at us kids in his class on the evils of divorce and the wickedness of being unfaithful. He was a mess." He picked up the pack of cigarettes and shook one out, the chains clinking.

Interviewer - "What happened?"

He put the cigarette in his mouth, lit it, took a deep drag, and then blew the smoke at the interviewer. "He killed her." He took another drag.

Interview - "When was the first time you killed something?"

He blew the grey smoke into the air and followed it with his eyes. "Birds." He nodded. "Baby birds in a nest. We put an m-80 in the nest and blew 'em up." He made the sound of an explosion and motioned the same with his hands. "Little feathers floating down. Birdie guts upon the ground. No more squawking, no more noise. No more wormies to enjoy." He smiled. "I made that up the same day. And what's worse? The other birds came and ate what was left of them. Cannibals."

Interviewer - "Did you feel bad?"

"About what? The birds?"

Interviewer - "Yes."

"No. Why would I? They're just animals."

Interviewer - "Animals are different than people?"

He scratched his head and looked at the man asking the questions. "Are you stupid? What kind of question is that?"

Interviewer - "Let me put it this way; did you feel bad when you killed the first person?"

He took another long hard drag and blew the smoke to the side. "No. He deserved it." He flicked the ash off the end of the cigarette onto the ground. "He was a bully. Bigger than everyone else in the school. Grade school. I liked this girl that sat two desks over from me on the right. She was a feisty little thing, stuck up for the kids that he pushed around. One day he shoved her down and pushed her face into the mud. I wanted to do something so bad but I couldn't move. He'd beaten the crap out of me several times." He rolled the cigarette in his fingers. "I hated him. And I hated the fear that had made it impossible for me to move or even speak. I watched in anger and disgust, I remember. Anger at him and disgust at me. He laughed at her when she got up. One boy stepped forward and the bully knocked him down and kicked him."

He took another drag and then flicked the ash off the cigarette, more out of habit than need. "I learned two very important things that day. One was the power of fear. The other was that you can defeat brute force and ignorance with forethought and intelligence. It took several weeks, but he got what he deserved. He liked to steal our lunches, so I made sure I sat next to him almost every day. I made out like I was trying not to be afraid of him, which got me beat up some more. But he would take my lunch every time." The prisoner laughed. "He got real sick, but he didn't die. I don't think they ever did find out why. Oh, how they all mourned for the worthless bully when he was in the hospital, even the kids that he had beat up and pushed around."

Interviewer - "How did he get sick?"

"Rat poison. Just a little at a time, but he was such a pig I doubt if he would have noticed a whole plate of it."

Interviewer - "And you didn't feel bad about it."

"Nope. Still don't."

Interviewer - "Did all your victims deserve it?"

"Victims. That's an interesting word isn't it?" He crushed the cigarette out in the ash tray. "A wife gets beat and abused for years, and when she kills the man, he becomes the victim. Hmmm. Interesting." He sat back and thought for a moment as he rubbed his chin. "Victims aren't always the ones that die. Yes, all my victims, as you put it, deserved it."

He smiled ever so slightly. "There was a lady in the neighborhood who yelled and scolded all of us kids for crossing her lawn or being too noisy. Her dog would bark like crazy when we would pass by. We'd tell the dog to shut up and she'd come unglued. We usually just avoided her.

"But one time my mother invited her over for some kind of neighborhood get-together and this old wind bag did nothing but put everyone down. My mother had made a baked ham and this nasty old lady told my mother that she would never eat anything that had pineapples on it. My mother handled her so graciously, but the old lady just kept up her railing on anything that belonged to the others.

"But these people were good people. So when her little dog came up missing and she was all distraught about it, they came to her side to comfort her. They brought her food and did her dishes and house work. And she ate her dog."

Interviewer - "What was that?"

"She ate her dog. My mother made some stew that she knew for sure the old hag would like, and when Mom wasn't looking, I put some of the little dog in that stew. So I guess she ate something she would never eat."

Interviewer - "Did you have a good childhood?"

"As good as anyone. My mother was divorced a couple times and my dad wasn't around much, but that was pretty much the norm where I grew up. Most of my friends had step-parents or single moms."

Interviewer - "Were you ever sexually assaulted?"

"Yeah, but that's not uncommon." He didn't want to talk about it.

Interviewer - "When you killed someone, was it power or retribution that motivated you."

"Hmm. Both, I think. Retribution provides the motive with anger at its core, where as power is driven by the desire to control. And to control another human being is the greatest form of power. To make another thinking, breathing human being do something that they don't want to do is a rush. Especially if it's something they swore they'd never do."

"The cities are the easiest place to find people on which to enforce your will. I blew a bunch of money in a bar one time just to draw attention to myself. Then I walked out into the darkest, dirtiest alley I knew of and sure enough some thug followed me." He laughed. "Listen, there are few things more pleasurable than to see a full grown man—a big man, tough guy, you know the type—to see him look at you with no respect and even with contempt. And then to see his face change in an instant when he looks down the barrel of a gun. All the BS macho attitude disappears like a whiff of smoke when he's confronted with the thought of dying right then and there. One guy peed his pants. Big guy, fat slob, looking to roll me, followed me into the alley. I acted like I was a little drunk and was taking a leak. He started giving me grief and I turned around with a .38 pointed between his eyes. He lost it right then and I knew I had him. Made him get on his knees, and then I made him lick the asphalt." He laughed. "He begged and pleaded until he made me sick of it. He was just another example of a pathetic hypocrite. I shot him in the back of the head."

Interviewer - "Weren't you worried about getting caught?"

"Not in that neighborhood. Cops don't go there unless it's the swat team. And there are no dots to connect, no drug deals, owed money or insurance, so no ties. The cops will take the first week to run down all the upstanding friends he didn't have and trace leads to all the drug deals and petty theft connections. By the next week they'll have another case with better leads, or at least hotter leads. They, the cops, don't have the time, man power, nor the inclination to find out who killed a piece of crap that rolled people for a living."

Interviewer - "What do think about the police?"

"Oh. That's half the fun. Without them it's like playing monopoly by yourself. They make it interesting. And entertaining I might add.'

Interviewer - "Entertaining?"

"Oh yeah. You get to watch them try to figure it all out while you look on from above, like watching mice in a maze. You know more than they know. You give them little clues that they have to run down, all leading to churches and shelters and, if it right, you can send them right back to their own cop shop. Throw a little cheese of doubt into the minds of people who think they're really smart and they'll build a house out of cheese."

He leaned forward and folded his arms on the table. "I sent news clippings and posted letters to the biggest, busiest cop shop you can find just to set them on the trail of something that hadn't happened yet." He sat back. "They were investigating a murder that I was going to commit. It was cool. Everything they read referred to the victim as already dead. The man left the country for six months." Again he smiled and laughed at his own accomplishments. "You see our society is a microwave society. We want it all right now. We don't want to wait. And when things don't happen we move on, when things do happen we forget real quick. I waited two years. Two years, before he died exactly how I had told the police he would."

Interviewer - "And how was that?"

"Let me fill you in. He was a fairly powerful individual, that's why the police could be so easily moved into action. He wasn't a back alley thug, but he was arrogant. No more than that, he was a classic case of narcissism. He was easily built up. He believed anything good about himself, but became vengeful at any and all criticism. Pride is a great motivator, but fear is the greatest motivator. And a man like this is afraid, afraid of criticism and failure, and what others say, They'll walk right over anybody to stay on top and to be the big man in the club.

"And here's the hook; they'll take credit for someone else's work every time. If someone pats them on the back for someone else's job well done, they'll eat it up, they'll lick the bowl. So that's where you lure them in. The notes I sent to the police were death threats on him, that made him feel real important, more important than he was, built up his ego. Then I sent emails to people who were on the fringe of his business but not directly connected. In a 'he said, she said" type rumor, I told them what wonderful things he was doing. Actual accomplishments that he was involved in but not fully responsible for.

"This starts making a few people upset, but they're either below him in the firm or even with him. As these outside people give him the credit, he's eats it up. Everything he's involved in gets out to a lot of people, as to the great job he did. I mean his social life, his business dealings—even if he attended an event that had a connection with a charity, he got the credit.

"Now he had just one man over him in the firm, Jenkins. He was a calm, cool individual. But the one thing he hated, someone taking credit for what he did and anyone trying to deal him dirt from under the deck. But that's not the line that brings it in. You see, Jenkins has ties with some real bad dudes, the type that don't allow dealing bottom cards. And that was the angle. I start making it look like he's moving money around behind Jenkins' back. I faked a Swiss bank account and let things slip out to the right people. I would drop hints here and there about big deals going on. And then I make sure it comes around to the head man, that this guy is working deals behind his back. And, he's getting credit for the boss's work. Not good.

"Of course, he denies it, but it all looks too fishy for the big guy. So I put the finishing touch on it by calling the head man's girl on this guy's phone. Then the head man's main clients call and say they've been approached by this arrogant jerk. These clients are big money with the bad dudes." He looks at the interviewer. "You staying with me?"

Interviewer - "Yes. I'm with you. It looks like the arrogant man, that you obviously don't like, is trying to undercut his boss, who's tied in with the ah, bad dudes, and now it looks like he's going for the boss's girl. Is that about it?"

"Yeah. You're on it. So this man, that I don't like—"

Interviewer - "Why don't you call him by name?"

"I don't know. I don't want to."

Interviewer - "Okay."

"So the boss gets a list of things that this guy's been up to. Of course I made most of it up, but there's enough truth in it to make it believable and piss him off. Big money deals under the table combined with the fact that his girl is getting messages from this guy." He smiled. "He lost everything. First his job, then his reputation, and then his wife—everything fell apart at the seams, crumbled right out from under him.

How embarrassing for such an upstanding citizen."

Interviewer - "How did you get all this done? How did you get access to his files and things?"

"He was my step-dad. Worthless jerk. All nice and respectable in public but beat the crap out of my mom at home and treated me like I was scum."

Interviewer - "What about women? Did you ever marry? Girlfriends? Dating?"

"Ah women. What an enigma they are. They work so hard to gain power over the very thing they want to protect. There's a force that drives them to dominate a man and then if they do, they have no respect for him. The more they beat him down, the less respect. And the woman getting treated like a dog waits on that scum hand and foot. Women are screwed up."

He shifted in his chair. "But I like the women. Oh yeah. I guess that's man's downfall, hmm. Trying to live with a crazy person and call it normal. I've had lots of girlfriends. I mean, I'm no Casanova, but I'm not ugly either. I've had my share of women." He nodded with a satisfied look. "One girl I lived with for a while was flat nuts. I mean crazy. She was punked out one day and then Goth the next. You never who was going to be showing up. But talk about wild in bed, man! She'd bust you up, she liked it rough too.

"We got going one night and she wanted me to choke her. I didn't want to at first, but then she, well, she persuaded me to get crazy with her. So I did. It was a rush. Man what a rush. About a month later we were playing our game and," he paused, "and I couldn't stop. I couldn't make my fingers let go. She was all into it and then she got scared. I could see it her eyes. The fear, pure unadulterated fear. I had never seen fear in her eyes before. She was the dominating type, but now she was afraid. That rude, controlling, forceful woman, was absolutely scared to death. And then it just...went away."

Interviewer - "Was that the first time?"

He nodded. "Yeah." He reached for the pack of smokes with the familiar clinking. "No one even asked about her. No one came looking for her. She was just gone. It was like she had just walked out the door and after a while I didn't miss her either."

Interviewer - "But you liked it."

"Yeah." He lit the smoke, took a deep drag, held it for a second and let it out. His whole body relaxed. "I never got into drugs. Didn't do it for me you know. I drank quite a bit, but I wasn't an alcoholic by any means. Porn was alright, but it got old quick. Gambling didn't make any sense at all. Money was a means to an end, just needed it like everyone else. But that look of fear, that—that's a rush."

Interviewer - "Just women?"

"No. Oh no. Fear in a man's eyes is a whole other ball game. It's not hands on like a woman; you can see it better from a few feet away. With hands on they think they have a chance, you never see the fear. It's when they can't lay a hand on you, that drives it through the roof. In their mind, if they could just get one hand on you they'd tear you to pieces, they'd rip your heart out. But they can't, they're helpless. And for some this isn't enough to drive them over the edge. Some need a—a little more incentive, shall we say. Something dear to their heart, then you'll see fear. Helpless, hopeless fear." He took a drag and then exhaled. "But if they live through it they die before they die. The life just goes out of them. It's more of a mercy killing at that point. In fact they want it by then."

Interviewer - "Did you look for certain people or just happen upon them?"

He blew a smoke ring into the air and pointed at it with his shackled hands. "Look at that." He smiled. "It just happened. See someone on the street, they catch your eye. At first you just notice them, and then you start to watch them. Then you can't stop watching." He sat up again and leaned forward on the table. "It becomes a challenge—to follow them, track them, to see without being seen. If you can follow them home then game on. No, it's not just following someone. No, it's a study. You learn their habits and their tendencies and who their friends are and how many kids, if they have kids. Are they married? Do they have a steady boyfriend? Are they cheating on their husband? That's a good one. You should see the mess you can make when you come across that little bit of information. The cops go after the poor husband every time." He laughed. "He gets cheated on and then arrested for murder. Bad day."

He flicked the ash off. "But to watch and study them is like therapy. It's calm and quiet and peaceful as they go about their business without a single thought that someone is watching them. Then, depending on how boring or exciting their life is, you drop a hint. Just a subtle little something. You don't want to give up too much, just make them wonder for a moment. Not too long, just a thought, just a thought that something's wrong, then leave it be and watch. Then push it a little more and watch them start to squirm. They'll be accused of being paranoid and jumping at shadows, when all along they were right."

He looked at the interviewer. "Did you know that man is the only creature that ignores his instincts? Did you know that? If an animal is frightened of something you can't make them go near it. They'll fight tooth and nail and by no means will they go willingly. But a person will talk themselves right out of what their gut tells them is no good.

"When they start looking around because they feel like they're being watched, that's when it gets good. You can see the nervousness in their eyes and in their actions. They'll try to shake it off, but they can't. They look around when they're unloading the groceries in the driveway, or when they're in the hallway of their apartment building. It's funny, but when they're around a lot of other people, they don't feel it as much. It's when they're alone that they can feel it, when they're at home."

Interviewer - "What's the longest amount of time that you've watched someone?"

"A year." He put the smoke in his mouth and scratched his head with a clinking sound. "She became my, ah…hobby, I guess you could say. I remember the first time I saw her. It was in the grocery store. I was there getting some ice cream one night. It was late—ten, ten-thirty. I was leaving the store and she was coming in. I saw her and walked on by. Then I turned and looked back, but went on out. I was ready to leave, but I just sat there in my car and waited to watch her come out. The longer it took, the more determined I became, the more I wanted to see her walk out the doors. Then I asked myself, 'I wonder what kind of car she drives?'. So now I had to wait and find that out. Thirty minutes later I was driving by her house as she ran inside to get out of the rain. That's right, I remember now, it was raining and pitch black outside. The hedge on the right side of her house was tall and thick and there were no lights."

He looked to the interviewer. "Most people would go right then and try to take a look, but that's why they get caught—in too big of a hurry. You have to take your time, think it out. Remember what I said, 'Forethought and intelligence over brute force and ignorance.' They're not going anywhere, they live there." He raised a finger. "And no pictures! Stupid idiots take pictures."

Interviewer - "What about kids?"

"Perverts, those guys are sick. Kill 'em, cause you can't cure 'em. Those child molesters have ruined more lives and screwed up more people than anything else in the world." He stuck his finger out and thumb up in the symbol of a gun and pointed it at the interviewer. "Boom. Done deal. No fuss, no muss. They ought to keep them locked up when they catch them. They broke the law, punish them."

Interviewer - "What do you think about the laws?"

He took a long drag and blew it out. "I like them, I think they need more."

Interviewer - "More?"

"Absolutely. The more laws they have, the more work for the police to do. The more jammed up the system gets, the less time they have to work their cases, and the more freedom for the smart guys. They spend thousands of hours on dumb criminals and accidental crimes."

Interviewer - "Accidental crimes?"

"Yes. Law abiding citizens that break laws that they have no idea exists. Some cop with a high IQ has to prove himself to the average hard working Joe going to work just how smart he is. Harassing the good guys because the good guys won't pop him in the head. Punks with a badge. If they weren't wearing a uniform, they'd be getting beat up. You'll never see these guys in the dangerous situations, or doing undercover work. But that's okay because they're catching those dangerous speeders doing eight miles over the speed limit."

He smirked. "The more laws there are, the better it is for the criminals because they're not following the laws anyway, are they? So it puts more burdens on the people that do, and the ones trying to enforce the laws. It takes the pressure off the guys that don't care about the laws."

Interviewer - "You don't hate the law or the police?"

"Nah. Some of the people that are in the system are stupid jerks, but you find that anywhere you go. In every job you've got idiots."

Interviewer - "Did you have trouble holding down a job?"

"Not at all. Did the work, didn't make a fuss. Had no desire to be a boss, so I didn't step on anybody's toes. Just went to work, showed up on time, and kept my mouth shut. No big deal."

Interviewer - "Did you ever have a run-in with a co-worker?"

He crushed the smoke out. "Once. He was a lead man over about twelve of us. Arrogant jerk. He'd create problems to fix just to make himself look better. Never gave credit to anyone but him. Nobody could do anything right, we were all stupid. He had just a little touch of the inferiority complex going on. Worried that we were all after his meaningless little job." He laughed and then looked at the interviewer. "Rumors. That's all it takes to destroy another person. Not complete falsehoods—your target has to be associated with the incident, the closer the better.

"I would just drop little tidbits of half-truths here and there, just planting the seed of doubt. Now because the boss of the boss isn't willing to readily admit that they made a mistake, they are a long time in coming to the conclusion that their 'prodigy' is a screwup. So once again you have to take your time, be patient, and basically let them hang themselves."

Interviewer - "What kind of things would you say to set this up?"

"Well, every boss has an ego, and when you poke that sensitive little tender spot long enough, you'll get results. But first you have to alienate the target from anyone below them. Leave them no allies to come to their aid. Prideful people are easy to manipulate. Just build them up in the direction that will do the most harm. Put down their boss to them, which they will readily agree that 'they' are better qualified to be boss. Start rumors about employees badmouthing them—which again, because of their inferiority issues, they will believe. It's all about picking the right issues and the timing. Within a year you can turn almost anyone against anyone else, but you have to remain in the background. It's not about you, remember, it's all about them. Keep it about them and let someone else gloat in the turmoil and downfall that follows. Poison ivy in bloom is a dangerous wallflower."

Interviewer - "What happened to him?"

"Lost his job." He shrugged. "People are easily trapped in the same way animals are. Animals have needs and if you use those needs you can capture or kill them. An animal needs food and water. Set a trap or wait for them at either of those places and they will come. People are much the same, but they have needs beyond food and water: things like pride and ego, affection and love, the need to be needed, the want to be wanted. These are watering holes and bait that capture people all the time."

Interviewer - "Is it fun for you? To do this to people?'

He searched for the right word. "It's justice, they deserve it. They treat people like inferior human beings, so I just do to them what everybody else wants to do; bring them down."

Interviewer - "I notice that you don't swear or use foul language. How come?"

He shifted in the chair. "My mother swore a lot, and it always bothered me that she did. It made her less than she was. She was a loving caring person but when she cursed and swore it made her look cheap and raunchy, like the women on the street."

Interviewer - "How many husbands did your mother have?"

"Just two."

Interviewer - "How many boyfriends lived in your home when you were growing up?"

"I don't know. Half a dozen, maybe more counting the weekend flings and one night stands."

Interviewer - "Did that bother you?"

"I don't know. I didn't like very many of them. I always thought she was better than that. I guess maybe I thought better of her than she thought of herself."

Interviewer - "Did you know your father?"

"Yeah. He didn't have much time for me. We went fishing once; that was cool. He took me out on a boat that a buddy of his had, and we caught a bunch of fish. We had to hide them because we were over the limit. We had a fish in the glove box of the truck." He laughed. "His buddy threw it in there at the last minute because a warden was coming. That was a fun day." He had a faraway look in his eye. "Didn't see much of him after that. I tracked him down when I turned twenty-one. Spent a week at his place, but that was the last time that I spent any amount of time with him. We drank a lot, went to some bars. He picked up a woman and brought her home with us, an old girlfriend or something. I dropped in on him every now and then, but only for a few hours or so, never more than a day."

Interviewer - "Did you like him?"

"I guess so. Yeah, I was just disappointed I guess. I thought we should have been closer, but I don't know why I thought that. None of my friend's dads were around. Maybe I got the idea from TV or the movies or something. Maybe even from church."

Interviewer - "You mentioned church a couple of times. How long did you go to church?"

"My mother sent me to a church in our neighborhood. I guess she thought it would do me some good, or maybe she was trying to make up for what she was lacking. Her parents were fairly religious people, and she grew up in church, so maybe she sent me there out of guilt. I went for about four years, maybe five. By high school I was done with that stuff."

Interviewer - "Did you believe any of it?"

"Some. Not all. There were things that the preachers and teachers would say about the Bible that didn't fit or make sense. But I guess at that time I did believe it. I remember really trying to do what they said, to be good and not sin, to make the right choice every time." He shrugged. "I just gave up on it after a while. If I had to follow all the rules to get to heaven, then I guessed I was going to hell, and I wasn't going to feel miserable and guilty my whole life for not being good enough. So I went the other way, it was a lot easier, I can tell you that. At least I knew I was wrong. After awhile the guilt subsides and you forget about all that guilt crap they put on you."

Interviewer - "You mentioned something about justice. Do you believe in justice?"

"Oh yeah. There is justice for everyone, I have no doubt. It just doesn't come when and where we want it." He paused. "Unless you take it for yourself, on purpose. People sit around and complain about how unfair things are when bad people get away with bad things and yet they do nothing about it but sit around and complain. They gripe about the injustice in this world, but do nothing to right the wrongs that they see. They deserve to wallow in their self-pity and sit in the stink of fear that binds them to inability to do something. They wait for the law, or worse, the government, to do something about the wrong that is plainly seen and flaunted in front of everybody. Those that hide behind the letter of the law are simply smarter than the average citizen. They actually know the laws that are meant to control them. Therefore, they avoid the conviction or the hard time because they walk that line. Just enough to create," he raised his hands in the motion of making quotes, "'reasonable doubt.'" He laughed. "When you're waiting for an unjust government to correct unjust acts of others, you'll have a long wait."

Interviewer - "I thought a corrupt government readily went after others that were corrupt. Perhaps in the ultimate show of hypocrisy."

"At first, yes." He leaned forward. "They readily attack others with vigor and enthusiasm, but when they themselves are continually exposed, especially if they have any connection at all with what they would persecute, they'll start to back off. They begin to turn their eye away from injustice. They will create issues that are not easily proven wrong. Remember what I said about rumors? The government is better at that game than anyone. No different than those worthless churchgoers. Preach fear, and then sell the solution. The ignorant, lazy people of this country will eat it up—no, not eat it up, they buy it up." He sat back. "Fear is the greatest motivator on the face of the earth."

Interviewer - "Greater than love?"

"Yes. Love runs a close second, but fear is greater. For fear of a child being hurt, a mother will stand between the child and an abusive father. For fear of losing a home, someone will subject themselves to the abuse of an arrogant jerk of a boss. For fear of rejection, someone will walk right past the very person they think they love. For fear of failure, people refuse to try something new. Fear forces people into submission to the rulers and authorities that oppress and victimize them. Fear keeps men paying money to the very people that are controlling them. Fear, my friend, controls the very nature of the human soul. Fear, not love."

Interviewer - "What are you afraid of?"

"Nothing. That's what gives me freedom."

Interviewer - "You're not afraid to die?"

"Everybody dies. It's the illusion people create within themselves that they aren't going to die that creates the fear of death. They block it out and put it off, so that they don't have to think about it, therefore they don't have to deal with it. But they will, eventually. And when it comes, if it doesn't come in a flash, they'll be dead in a very short time."

Interviewer - "What do you mean?"

"You've heard about people that seem to be healthy and in good shape and then they're told they have cancer or something like that. Within a month they look dead and soon after they are?"

Interviewer - "Yes."

"They never thought about dying, at least when the subject was about them. Death happened to other people and that was okay, they had pushed it so far back in their mind, it just somehow didn't apply to them. When it does, they have an inward mental breakdown. They die long before they take their last breath. It's because the unthinkable has happened to them, and they don't know how to deal with it."

Interviewer - "So you're saying you're prepared for eternity?"

"I deserve whatever I get. That's what I'm saying."

Interviewer - "Are your mother and father still alive?"

"No. They're both gone."

Interviewer - "May I ask how?"

He grabbed up the pack of smokes once more and shook one out. For the first time he looked a little nervous. "My father died drunk and broke, just like he lived." He lit the cigarette and took a long, hard drag.

"No surprise to anyone that knew him. There were four people at his funeral, counting the preacher. I remember thinking what a waste of life his was. The days of his life ebbed away like the rotting of a dead log until finally nothing was left. He was just waiting for time to run out." He shook his head, stuck the cigarette in his mouth with clinking of chains, and then added. "But aren't we all."

He took the cigarette from his mouth and blew another smoke ring, but didn't point it out like the first one. "I often think, what made him such a looser? Why did he give up on living the way he did? He had no hope in his eyes, none at all. He just died. No cancer, no disease, and no hope."

Interviewer - "If you knew what made him that way, would you have tried to help?"

He shrugged. "I like to think I would have, but I don't know for sure. I think I would have liked to have tried to help him. What could take away a man's very will to live? He didn't have any fear either." He looked at the interviewer. "When you don't fear death, not much is left to fear. But what I don't understand is that for as long as I can remember, he never lived."

Interviewer - "Was he abusive?"

His eyebrows furrowed and his left eye twitched as he stuck the cigarette in his mouth and drew a long deep breath of smoke. He closed his eyes, held it for a second and then let it out. "I remember he worked at a packing house for a while. He put in long hard days cooped up inside a cinderblock building surrounded by blood and guts, bawling animals, and the smell of death. But it didn't seem to bother him, he was glad to have the job. 'Work's work' he used to say.

"Then Mom and him started fighting one day and then he was gone. That's when the other men started showing up. She wouldn't let them stay all night at first—they'd just stay late and leave. Then they started staying the night when I was gone, over at a friend's house or something. She talked like they hadn't stayed overnight, but she knew I knew. I guess she felt guilty, but it wasn't long before she stopped trying to hide it. They began staying weekends and then they would move in for a while."

He flipped the ash from the end of the cigarette. "Maybe that's what happened to Dad. Maybe she hurt him real bad." He looked at the interviewer. "Can someone care that much about someone else that they lose their will to live?" He shook his head. "Maybe Dad was weaker than I thought, or at least weaker than I thought he should be." He took another drag.

Interviewer - "Does that make you angry?"

"Hmm. Never thought about it that way. I don't know. Could be. Maybe if he would have been stronger he could have... No. He couldn't stop what she did."

Interviewer - "Does that make him weak?"

"No. I suppose not. But he should have been able to—to, I don't know! Do something! Not just leave, run away, afraid." He crushed out his cigarette. "I think were done for today. Guard!"

Interviewer - "Okay. Can I come back tomorrow?"

"Sure. I ain't going anywhere, yet." He grinned and sat back in the chair. "See you tomorrow."

****

The interviewer wore his reading glasses as he sat in the darkened room, with just a single lamp on beside him. The book was opened before him and a drink sat on the table with the lamp. A dark wooden desk sat off to his right and the wooden shelves were lined with books. The leather cushioned chair he sat in was his favorite and a picture of George Washington on bended knee hung on the wall. His mind rambled on in thoughts about the day and the man he had visited. Then the voice came, not an audible voice for others to hear, but loud and clear in his mind. A heavy voice, thick with guilt and condemnation, yet smooth and enticing. It came once more to reason with him on the issues at hand, about the things he had said or done or was about to do.

"What are you doing, Joe, going to see a man like that?" The voice of enticement whispered in his inner ear. "A murderer and a liar, a coward at best, the very type of person you loathe. Weak and vile, full of excuses. You heard the excuses, didn't you? 'Poor me, what a bad childhood, full of abuse and mistreatment.' Those are his excuses for what he's done. You know better than that. He's just another man that

24

chooses to continue to do wrong and then blame others for his actions. A weak, pathetic sinner."

"Aren't we all?" Joe replied out loud. "I am no better."

Enticement chuckled softly. "Now, now. Don't be so dramatic. You've never killed anyone, not even in war. You've never been to war, remember. And your childhood wasn't all that bad either, was it? No, you're not like him at all. He said it himself, he deserves everything he gets. You're not a sinner like that. You've never done the things he's done."

Joe picked up the glass and took a sip. "But if I were judged by my thoughts, I'm worse. And because I never acted on my thoughts, I'm probably more of a coward than he."

Enticement replied sarcastically. "Okay, whatever you say. If it makes you feel better thinking you're worse than that liar and murderer, then you go on thinking that. But we know better, don't we?"

Another voice interrupted. A strong, stern, calm voice with authority that was clear and full of life. "Enough," this voice said quietly. It then asked, "Do you trust me?"

"Yes," Joe replied. "Yes I do."

"Go back," Authority said.

"Okay," Joe answered and took another sip. He closed his eyes and laid his hand on the book in his lap. A smile came across his face, a smile that laughed at the efforts of the other voice and at his own doubts that opened the door for those thoughts.

The next morning, the interviewer sat with his cup of coffee and read from the book he loved so much. However, his thoughts rambled off so often that he finally gave up and stepped outside for a breath of fresh air. The heavy voice came again, but with condemnation.

"Who are you to try and help others? What wisdom do you hold that is going to enlighten troubled souls? How arrogant can you be, to assume that you have the power to lift others from the troubles of life? Have you forgotten your own sins and weaknesses? You know your failures and faults and yet you go to others as if you have all the answers. What a hypocrite."

Joe sipped his coffee and closed his eyes. That's when the other voice interrupted once again, the voice of peace.

"Be still," Peace said softly with power and assurance.

Joe sighed and relaxed.

****

The chains jingled and clinked as he shuffled into the room and sat down. "You came back. I'm a little surprised, I have to say."

Joe - "Good morning, Mr. Chambers. And why are you surprised?"

"It's just plain Eric." the prisoner said.

"Okay, Eric. Why didn't you think I'd be back? I said I would."

Eric -"Well, if I walked out of here I sure wouldn't come back." He smiled at the new pack of smokes on the table. "Thanks," he tapped the pack against his left hand. "I just don't understand why a guy like you would choose to spend time in this place with a guy like me, that's all."

Joe - "Just curiosity. This is the first time you've been in prison, isn't it?"

Eric -"Yeah. I had never even been in a local jail." He laughed and opened the cigarettes. "Go figure. Makes you wonder though, don't it?"

Joe - "About?"

Eric - "About how many others are out there that don't have a record or rap sheet. Just floating around, free as a bird, unnoticed and ignored by everyone." He lit a cigarette, took a hard drag, and held it before speaking again. "Going about their business just as polite and nice as can be, until they end up in your bedroom one night. You wake up and see a man standing over you that you may or may not know. It's your worst fear come to life. The most vulnerable place in the world is right there in the security of your own home. The one place you find comfort and solace from this cruel world and it's been invaded. Your sanctuary has just been defiled and desecrated. It is the ultimate act of invasion, it's power over someone else." He smirked. "It's fear."

Joe - "You said yesterday that you watched a woman for a year. Is that all you did?"

Eric - "Yes. Well, not exactly. I watched her, studied her, and even began to like her. She was single, no steady boyfriend, although she had several men in her life within that year. But they never spent the night with her. And they were nice guys too. She ran every morning unless the weather was too bad. When that was the case, she used the treadmill. She was twenty-six years old and liked to read novels, romantic fiction mostly, some biography, but mostly fiction."

He took another drag and blew the smoke into the air. "She had two very good friends, girlfriends. That's who she hung out with most of the time, if she went out. She worked in an office downtown, a receptionist at first, but quickly moved into the accounting department. Very smart young lady." He took another drag. "She liked red wine, chocolate covered caramels, fried egg sandwiches and milk, and she liked pickles too. Dill pickles right out of the jar." He looked up at the grey ceiling above. "Coffee every morning at the same little coffee house, lunch at the same little restaurant every day, chicken salad, nails every second Thursday at five, laundry on Wednesdays and the book store at least every other month." He put the cigarette in his mouth and thought for a moment. "She liked tea on Sundays." He let the smoke fall from his mouth along with the air he slowly loosed from his lungs.

Joe - "You know more about her than most men know about their wives."

Eric - "Sad, eh?"

Joe - "Why?"

Eric - "Why put so much time and effort into someone that doesn't know you exist?" He grinned and shook his head. "But it's really not that uncommon for people to pay a lot more attention to what they don't have than what they do. Wouldn't you agree?"

Joe - "Yes, I would."

Eric - "People always want what they don't have. Always looking into the neighbor's yard and over the back fence. Comparing themselves to everyone else and never satisfied for more than a moment. The human species is never content, not with what they have or what they are. They have an appetite that is never satisfied. Not with food, sex, possessions, money, power, nothing puts an end to the wanting."

He flicked the ash off the end of his cigarette. "I heard about a study one time that asked the question, 'Would you rather make one hundred thousand dollars a year while everyone you know makes fifty thousand a year, or, would you rather make two hundred thousand a year while everyone you know makes three hundred?' Do you know what they choose? That's right: the majority chose the one hundred thousand over the two hundred. Unbelievable."

Joe - "But doesn't a dog guard his dish even after he's eaten all he can? Or bury as many bones as he can get even though he'll never find them again?"

Eric - "Hmmm. You have a point. Maybe it's just the animal instinct in us. A survival mechanism that accompanies our desire for self preservation." He thought for a second on the new angle of human nature. "Actually that makes sense. Look at women that dress, talk and act in a manner that draws the attention of men. It's not that men don't notice them, because we both know that all a woman has to do is show up and men will notice. But it's the competition with the other women that prompts the behavior, the need to be chosen, singled out from the rest of the flock."

He grinned. "Look at a dog in heat, or a horse. They can make a stud go brain dead in a quick hurry. But it's the males of this world that strut and parade and fight for attention from the females of their speices, from the forked horn buck to the prairie chicken. So it is with men and women of the human kind. Women dress up, or down, to get the most attention from the men that are butting heads with each other to get the attention of the women. What a spectacle we make of ourselves. When all we have to do is say something even remotely intelligent to one another and see if there's an attraction beyond the eyes."

Joe - "Sounds like you studied the situation."

Eric - "You could say that." He nodded. "It's like playing poker."

Joe - "What is?"

Eric - "People. In a poker game you watch for people to give their hand away by the way they act. So it is when you watch people, men or women. If you're watching, not just looking, you can see what's in their head. What they like and dislike, which tells you what they'll do next. Besides the fact that we are creatures of habit. It isn't all that hard to find out all you want to know about someone."

Joe - "Whatever happened to the woman you watched for a year?"

Eric - "Do you know she was the only person I ever knew that wasn't a hypocrite? At first it was just a matter of waiting for her to give up her real life, her secrets. The part of her that nobody knew about or at least the part she didn't want certain people to know. Everybody has something, except her. She was exactly what she seemed to be." He shook his head. "No lies, no hidden life, no falseness about her. I think," he pondered his words for a moment, "I think she is probably the only honest person there ever was. Only one I ever met anyway."

Joe - "You met her?"

Eric - "Yes I did. More than once in fact." He flicked an ash off. "Had coffee with her a few times. Just an acquaintance as far as she knew. Met her friends too, nice girls, for the most part, not as nice as her though. They were a bit flirty, vain and superficial. Placed a lot of value in what they looked like."

Joe - "Don't most women?"

Eric - "I suppose so, but some more than others. Most everyone cares about how they look, but for some people it's what gives them any value whatsoever. It's not that they want to look good, they need to look good." He put the cigarette in his mouth and shifted in the chair. With the cigarette still in his mouth he said. "You know there's a difference between need and want." He took the cigarette out and blew the smoke into the air. "People can want a lot of things but that doesn't necessarily change their behavior. They just go on with their lives wanting it. But needing something, that's a whole other matter all together. Needing things is when people alter their lives in order to get it. They subject themselves to things they swore they wouldn't. When you need something, you give that thing, whatever it is, power over yourself. Power over your reasoning and the choices you make. The thing you need becomes your god.

And then that thing has to fulfill the obligations of a god, it has to be perfect. Be it man, woman, or child. They have to be perfect because you have placed them in the position of fulfilling your life. Then you'll hate them for it, because now they control your very thoughts." He laughed. "I've seen it. People end up hating the very thing they loved; first, because it fails them and then, because it controls them. What a vicious cycle."

Joe - "Did you go to college?"

Eric - "No. I just read a lot. Well, I used to read a lot. I read when I can now, which isn't as much as I would like. There's a lot of information out there for anyone who wants to look for it. But mainly it's just common sense: watch people and learn. Really, if you just ask why, that will put you on the path of discovery. But most people don't want to know why, especially when it come to themselves. They're happy in their little make believe world of lies and denials."

Joe - "So why did you watch her?"

Eric - He flicked another ash off his smoke and nodded. "Hmm. I avoided that question as much as possible. But there was something fulfilling in it. It was a relationship, as odd as that sounds, but without the—well, without the chance rejection."

Joe - "Whatever became of it, your relationship?"

Eric - "I had been watching her for about year, like I said, and knew her intimately, but had never dropped a hint that would have made her nervous, or scared. Then one night a guy drove by for the third time that evening. He came back the next night and the next. The third night he slipped in between her house and the hedge. He watched her through the window off and on for a couple of weeks. Then one night when she was out with her friends, he went in the house and through her bedroom. It was only a matter of time before he would harm her. He was moving way too fast and needed to push it. He needed more, you could tell.

Eric crushed the cigarette out. "I checked him out and found his police record and a trail of accusations where ever he had been. Number one rule, keep a low profile, don't draw any attention to yourself. So what do I do? Call the cops and tell them that I was watching a guy watch a girl? Yeah? Don't think so! He went in one night and waited for her to come home, I waited and watched. He came out around two in the morning. I waited and watched until she got up. He was coming to the end of his thrill ride. He had pushed it as far as he could without her knowing it. Now she was looking around like someone was watching her and getting nervous.

I broke into his apartment and found all the tell tale signs of your common watcher: photos, hand written notes, her mail and personal possessions and trophies of his previous victims. He was getting very close to the end of the game. He would be making his presence known within the next two weeks. And then he'd kill her, after he terrified and molested her."

Joe— "And that bothered you?"

Eric - "Yes. Yes, it did."

Joe - "Why?"

Eric took a deep breath and then let out a heavy sigh as he crushed out his smoke. "I liked her. She was the only honest person I have ever met. I said that already, didn't I? Well, it's true. She didn't deserve what this guy was going to do to her. If I waited for him to make his move, she would never be the same again. She would spend the rest of her life being afraid of what was behind the door.

"He had killed before and was brutal in his methods. He liked to make them beg, he took pictures of them when they were at their lowest point, and after. He would pull every ounce of life from her soul before he took it from her body."

Eric was looking down at the concrete floor in deep thought, and then he looked up at Joe with a dead calm stare in his eyes and a smirk on his face. His voice lost the flippant charm and sarcasm and became a cold whisper. "I waited for him. Just like he had waited for the others, and how he would wait for her. In the shadows of the night, in the darkest shades of black, I waited for him. He would come in and go to the kitchen, pour a drink, sit and watch TV for a while. Then he would go to his trophy room and examine his past conquest to gain motivation for the deeds to come.

"It was four in the morning when I stood over him while he slept. I stared at him without moving and watched him breathe in and out in perfect rhythm. He twitched and shifted under the covers, then blinked. His eyes opened for a moment and then closed, then opened again. He stared up for a second and then closed them, processing what he knew he hadn't seen. It must be a dream, a nightmare. He held his breath and opened them again. He wasn't dreaming, it wasn't a nightmare—there was a man in his room standing over him.

"He didn't move or even breathe, because he had been on the other side of this scenario. He tried not to show the fear in his heart, but I could see it; I could feel it. He was afraid, afraid of dying. His breathing began to quiver as I leaned down, locking his eyes to mine, and whispered, 'You'll never frighten anyone again.' His eyes widened as the straight razor swiftly sliced the skin on his throat—through the trachea tube and carotid artery, sending blood spurting everywhere. He grasped my wrist, but it was too late and he knew it. He reached for my face, but I moved just out of arms length as he grasped the air with his hand and gasped for breath with his mouth like a fish out of water."

Eric sat and stared at nothing for a long time before he reached for the pack of smokes again. He lit up and sat back with the same flippantly sarcastic look as before. "Thanks for the smokes, Joe. That's money in here."

Joe - "Not a problem. Why did you do it?"

Eric - "Like I said. She didn't deserve it."

Joe - "If I may make an odd observation…?"

Eric - "Sure." He shrugged.

Joe - "You have a very distinct opinion of right and wrong. Justice and injustice."

Eric - "Yeah, I guess you could say that. Most things are either right or wrong—there's not as much grey area as people like to think. But really, everybody has an opinion of right and wrong, it just differs from others."

Joe - "What happened to her?"

Eric - "I never went back. I walked away and never went back. She had no idea what had taken place. She probably wondered where certain articles of clothing had gone, why things were out of place now and then or why she had been feeling odd. But she'll forget about all that soon enough."

Joe - "I have to ask, how does that make you feel? When you can decide who lives and who dies."

Eric - "Smart." He nodded and pondered the question and the answer. "Yes, it makes you feel smart—smarter than the law, smarter than the courts, and smarter than the law abiding citizens. They watch murders walk away because they had really good lawyers, or because a cop messed up on the arrest or on a technicality knowing full well that the person is guilty." He leaned back and looked up at the grey ceiling. "I suppose there's a power element to it also. When a week goes by and the police have not kicked down your door, or even knocked on it, you believe you really are as smart as you like to think you are. And with that thought comes power, arrogance that you won't be challenged on your decisions." He sat forward and raised a finger. "But, you cannot cross the line that says you 'can't' be challenged! That's when you make mistakes, that's when you dare them to catch you and that's when they do catch you."

Joe studied the man across the table and watched how the man's personality altered with the situation he was speaking of. It was odd to see a convicted murderer have such a set and distinct opinion of right and wrong, although his convictions on the subject were mostly directed towards others.

Joe - "Would you like something to drink?"

Eric - "A bottle of Jack would be nice." He laughed. "Water, just water."

Joe got up and spoke to the guard through the narrow opening in the door then sat back down. "Do you miss her?"

Eric - "I did at first. But I got over it after a while. Sometimes I wonder whatever became of her."

Joe - "Did you watch as they investigated the, ah—the watchers case?"

Eric - "It was almost three weeks before anything was released on the news. I had almost forgotten about it. I can guarantee they didn't work very long or very hard on the case. When they found his room full of trophies, they pretty much walked away and chalked it up to a good thing for public safety and no cost to public funds in his defense."

The guard knocked on the door prompting Joe to get up and retrieve two bottled waters from the little window. He set one on the table in front of Eric, opened the other for himself. He handed both bottle caps back to the guard on the other side of the window.

Joe - "Did you ever get a chance to put all that time and effort into a wife or girlfriend?"

Eric - "Yes, I did. Met a woman a while later and began a great relationship with her. It was very satisfying and rewarding. We got along real well and didn't fight much either, spent a lot of time together. Mom liked her and we were making plans for a long future together." He smiled. "Hmmm. She was a lot of fun. She liked chocolate, but don't all women? A weekend beer drinker, and she could put 'em down. She liked tea, one sugar. Crazy for pasta and garlic bread. She had a collection of sweaters that would boggle the mind, but didn't go over the top on shoes. Great legs, and I loved it when she would pull her hair back in a pony tail. Didn't get carried away with make-up, but liked getting her nails done once a month and her hair every other month. Loved dogs and cats and romantic movies. And fast cars too. Modest with jewelry, didn't like to stand out too much. Called her mom and dad once a week, at least, and talked to her sister just as much. She was a truly happy person, yes, she was truly happy."

Joe - "How long were you together?"

Eric - "Five years. Five wonderful years."

Joe - "What happened?"

Eric - "She died." Every ounce of joy fell from his face and a cloud of gloom settled on him.

Joe - "May I ask how?"

Eric didn't answer right away. He sat in the silence of the grey room as the depression of thoughts weighed heavy on his mind. "A drunk driver." He said in an emotionless voice. "Ran a red light and smashed into the driver's side of her car." He paused with a blank stare. "She lay in the hospital for two weeks in nothing but pain. She would wake up and cry with pain so, they gave her morphine to take the pain away. But there was too much internal damage and she died."

Joe - "And the driver?"

Eric - "What do you think, he walked away."

Joe - "What did you do about it?"

Eric - "Nothing." He went deeper into his gloom of depression. "Nothing." He repeated through clinched teeth. "Absolutely nothing."

Joe - "Why not?"

Eric - "Too obvious. I would be the prime suspect and they'd catch me." He looked around the room in which sat, inside the maximum security prison. "I should have, I'm here anyway. I should have killed the worthless son of a—."

Joe - "Did you watch him?"

Eric - "No. If I would have started it, I would have finished it." He grabbed up the pack of smokes, lit one, and took a drag, letting the smoke shoot out of both his nose and mouth. "I should have. Of all the people, I should have. I hate myself because I didn't. I let the fear of getting caught keep me from carrying out the punishment that he deserved." He took another long hard drag and blew it out hard. "He would have suffered. He would have felt the pain she felt, but without the mind numbing morphine to subdue it. He would have begged for me to end it, to kill him." He rubbed his forehead. "The news said he had a string of DUI's on his record and he was back on the road. There's your justice system at work for you." He took another drag and blew it up to the ceiling. "Where would you start? The first judge that let him go? The first attorney? The second or third? Where would start and where would you end? With the fifth attorney that defended him, or the cop that walked him out of the jail house?" He shook his head. "I should have killed him."

Joe - "Would that have helped you through your sorrow?"

Eric - "Damn right it would have." He flicked the ash from the cigarette and looked off to his right. "I don't know. Maybe not, but he deserved to die no matter what."

Joe - "If you got out today what would you do?"

Eric looked up at Joe with a look that said he hadn't thought about that. He didn't answer immediately, but weighed out the scenario in his mind for a long drawn out minute. The options clicked by as he stared at Joe, a little upset at the question because it took some of the fire out of his hatred. He nodded and glared at the interviewer.

If he were set free this very day and went out and killed that man, he would be right back in this very spot awaiting execution. But if he didn't kill him he could remain free from the imminent prospect of death row. He wanted to say that he would kill the man, but he couldn't. He couldn't honestly say he would do it, knowing he'd come back here.

Joe - "Why wouldn't you do it?" Joe could see the man's dilemma. "Is freedom that precious?" Eric stared at Joe who remained calm and non-condemning. "Is it the fear of prison and death, or the want of freedom that makes you hesitate?" Joe asked in a very non-confrontational tone. He was asking because he wanted to honestly know, but the man couldn't answer. He was unable to honestly reply and felt trapped within the walls of his hatred and desires.

****

Joe found himself in the same leather cushioned chair within his office walls, the light from the one lamp on the small table with the drink, the book in his lap and his glasses on. Looking at all the books on the shelves, he was trying to remember what they contained when they heavy voice of human reason gently spoke into his inner ear.

"Some people can't be helped. You know that. Some are doomed from birth to show the consequences of sin. Right? You can't change the destiny of another human being that is doomed by their own choices. It's not even the sins of his mother and father, it's his own admitted acts against helpless unarmed people. Why do you suffer for the sins of another man, especially someone like him?"

Joe picked up the drink, swirled it around in the glass and then spoke out loud. "Everyone suffers. Knowing why and not knowing why is the only difference."

Human reason chuckled softly. "I see. If you suffer enough then you can feel better about yourself, is that it? You can come home and not feel guilty about the people that are really suffering."

Joe took a sip from the glass. "We all have burdens to bear that are not of our choice, but they are for our good."

A weight of gloom began to settle down upon Joe's body and spirit. He took a deep breath, sighed and closed his eyes. The weight grew larger and pressed upon him as if he were being smothered by dark, damp dirt. It became heavier and heavier, causing Joe to hold his breath and then let it out, and then to take another and hold it as if he were actually trying to lift a large amount of weight that was stacked on his shoulders. The murky oppression wrapped itself around him with cold, dead fingers that pulled on his spirit.

"Dad." His daughter's voice pulled him from under the weight and the gloom lifted away. "Dad?"

"In here, Francine." He was weary, almost exhausted. He rubbed his hand over his face and set the glass down.

The slender twenty four year old with shoulder length brown hair and blue eyes walked into the dim lit room. She flipped the lights on, put her hands on her hips and scolded him. "Dad, what are you doing in here with the lights off again?"

He smiled. "I have a light on." He nodded towards the lamp on the table.

"Hmmm." She raised an eyebrow. "Right. I just dropped by to see how you were doing today."

"Thank you."

"And?"

He smiled and chuckled. "I'm doing just fine."

She sat down on the leather couch along the wall to his left and crossed her legs. "How's your interview going?"

"Good." He nodded, closed the book and set it on the table. "Interesting, to say the least."

"Does it bother you?" she asked. "Knowing all the things he's done?"

"I'd be lying if I said no. But what's more troubling is the fact that beneath what we know on the surface, there's a man with feelings, good and bad, emotions, even heartaches. That's hard to believe."

"I do find that hard to believe. So I'll just take your word on it." She smiled with a doubtful look. "What are you doing for dinner?"

"Oh, I'll fry up a steak or something."

"Right. More than likely you'll sit right here in your little think tank and contemplate the good and evil that's fighting over this world."

He frowned at the daughter who knew him too well.

She stood up. "Come on, get your coat, we're going out to eat." She walked over and took his hand. "We'll let someone else fry up that steak. Come on."

2

"Hey, Joe." The man opened the door of his house. "Come in." He swung the screen door open and Joe followed him inside, closing the door behind him. The man walked on into the kitchen. "Coffee's hot."

"Good," Joe answered as he made his way into his friend's kitchen. "I can always use a cup of hot coffee."

"It's not that foo-foo stuff they give you downtown you know." Tom, a career police officer, pulled a cup from the cupboard.

"Even better." Joe sat down at the little kitchen table. "Good 'ol regular coffee is still my favorite, and I'll take it any way but cold. Can't stand cold coffee."

"I hear that, my friend." Tom poured the second cup, carried both to the table and sat down in the other chair. "Dad used to put a pinch of salt in the pot, back when we boiled it on the stove."

"Why'd he do that?"

"Don't know, said that's what his dad used to do." Tom took a sip. "How's it going out at the prison?"

"It's okay. Not what I expected." Joe sipped from his own cup.

"How so?"

"A little more human than I thought possible, for a cold blooded murderer."

Tom sipped and then nodded. "Even Hitler had his human moments."

"I suppose so." Joe turned the cup in his hands. "You've done a lot for me already, so I hate to ask."

"What is it, Joe?" Tom smiled. "If I can do it I will. You know that."

"Yes I do. And I don't want to misuse it."

"Don't worry about that. If I can't do it, I won't; if I can, I will. Simple as that. Now, what is it?"

"This guy's mother. Can you find out what happened to her? He avoids the issue and I'd just like to know why." He looked at the cup in his hand. "Might not make any difference at all, may not mean anything at all. But I'd just like to know."

"Sure. I'll see what I can find out. The captain has been pretty good about this whole thing. He won't mind me looking into it a little deeper." Tom looked directly at his friend. "You sure you're all right with this?"

"Yeah." Joe nodded. "I'm good. It gets a little tough, but it's not all that bad. I'll be fine."

"All right. I'll take your word on it." Tom tapped the table top. "I'll be praying for you."

"Good. 'Cause I need the prayer and you need the practice."

****

A prison guard escorted Joe to the iron gate where the next guard would escort him to the interrogation room. The first guard handed the pack of cigarettes to the next guard. As they start down the grey concrete floor, the iron gate shut behind them with a loud and solid clunk of steel against steel that echoed down the hallway.

Without looking the guard spoke up. "Morning, Joe."

"Good morning, Frank."

"I just finished your last book. It was good. Really good."

"Thank you. I appreciate that."

"How do you come up with all those ideas?" The guard shot a quick glance at him.

"A wild imagination."

"Well you had some pretty good twists in it. Kept me turning the pages."

Joe smiled. "That's what I was shooting for."

When they reached the cold room, the guard opened the door for Joe and handed him the pack of smokes. Joe stopped as he was about to step in and looked at the guard. "The only difference between a dreamer and a writer is the writing."

The guard smiled and nodded. "I guess so."

Joe could hear the footsteps echoing down the hall, and then the opening of the door as the convict was led in. Joe felt the darkness settle in the room; that unseen, cold, damp cloud of oppression. Frank held the man's arm securely and walked him over to the chair, not letting go until the man was seated. Then, with another guard standing by, Frank chained the prisoner to the chair leg, looked the situation over, and returned to the door. He looked at Joe, who gave him a nod, then left the room.

Eric smiled. "Afternoon, Joe."

"Good afternoon, Eric."

"You really should get a hobby, you know that?"

"You're probably right about that." Joe smiled and slid the pack of cigarettes across the table.

"Thanks." Eric picked them up and smacked them against his left hand. "So what brings you back to this side of town?"

"Curiosity." Joe grinned.

"You do know what that did to the cat?"

"Yeah. Didn't turn out so well for him did it?"

"Nope." Eric pulled out a cigarette, then picked up the paper matches that had been with the pack of smokes.

"Has anybody else been here to see you?"

"Like who?"

"I don't know, your attorney?"

"My attorney? Ha." He took a drag on the smoke and blew it into the air. "The only reason he took my case was to get his face on TV."

"You pleaded guilty didn't you?" Joe questioned.

"That's because I was. Fact is I'm the only guilty man in here. Everyone else is innocent, just ask them." Eric laughed.

"I suppose you're right about that." Joe nodded.

Eric let the smoke roll from his nostrils and mouth. "Are you going to write a book about me?"

"Hmm. I wasn't planning on it. But you never know how things will work out."

Eric grinned. "Well if you do, use some of the money to upgrade my headstone, will ya'."

Joe raised an eyebrow. "Sure, I can do that."

"Then what exactly are you doing here?" Eric persisted. "Research on a coldblooded killer?"

"That's pretty much it. Like I said, I'm curious. Curious to know what makes people do what they do. As a writer I like to have reason behind characters, reason and thought. Not just random events clumped together."

"That helps to make a good book all right." Eric stuck the smoke in his mouth. "But it's not an easy thing to say why we do what we do, any of us."

"I would agree. Yet, on most of the bigger events of our lives, we had some forethought going into it."

"Really?" Eric cocked his head. "Like having babies?"

Joe frowned. "You have a point there."

"Men and women are hooking up all over the place with the hope of not creating life, and yet that's exactly what they do." Now Eric frowned. "Take that for instance. Why would a God of wisdom give stupid human beings the ability to create life? To bring forth another human being with no reason or forethought whatsoever? That, my friend, does not make sense."

"I cannot disagree with you on that subject. It is truly a mystery." Joe paused, then added, "But I guess it makes as much sense as the fact that we have the ability to take life, with no reason or forethought."

Eric looked at Joe with a thoughtful stare and exhaled. "Are we in the place of God?"

"I wouldn't go that far."

"We can create life and take life. Isn't that what God does? Isn't that his department?"

"Yes. That is his department." Joe hesitated for a moment. "But here's the other half of your mystery. Just because we have the ability to choose life or death does not mean that God is not in control."

Eric gave Joe a look of doubt. "And they call me crazy."

"No, they don't," Joe said, "that's why you're here."

"Oh yeah, that little detail." Eric smiled and took another drag.

"What did you do after your wife died?" Joe asked.

Eric lost his smile and looked away as he flicked off an ash. "That's when I started hanging out in the back alleys. Didn't much care who killed who." He looked back at the man across the table. "Found the closest city with the highest crime rate and went there."

"Did it help?"

"Help what?"

"Help the pain of your loss?"

"No, not really." Eric flicked the cigarette again, out of habit. "You married?"

"My wife died."

"How?"

"Cancer."

Eric took another drag. "That's as bad as a drunk driver."

Joe nodded. "I guess so, in some ways."

"But you can't forgive cancer, can you?"

The question caught Joe off guard. "Why do ask that?"

"Because you seem like the kind of guy that would forgive, or at least try to forgive, a drunk driver." He was watching Joe very closely. "Am I right?"

This time it was Joe who stared off at nothing. "I never thought about it like that."

"Maybe," Eric added, "the only difference is that the cancer in them dies with them. It doesn't walk away."

Joe looked at him. "I don't know if that helps."

"What did you do when your wife died?"

"I prayed," Joe answered. "I prayed before, during, and after."

"But it didn't help, did it?"

A faint smile came across Joe's face. "On the contrary, it helped a great deal."

Eric tilted his head back. "She still died?"

"Yes, she did. But like you said, we all die." Joe nodded. "The question we have to ask is, 'What then'?"

Eric returned the nod, but did not reply to the statement. Instead, he changed the subject. "Do you have any children?"

"Yes, a daughter."

"You must have a hard time even looking at me?" Eric flicked an ash.

"Hmm," Joe thought form a second. "At first, but not so much now."

"Why?"

"Not sure. Maybe you're more human than I wanted to believe."

"Well," Eric shifted in the chair, "don't let that rumor get out. It'll ruin my reputation. And maybe it just seems that way because I'm in chains."

"That could be," Joe replied. "That very well could be."

Eric sat up and looked Joe directly in the eyes. "I'll do as many interviews as you want Joe. But on one promise."

"And what might that be?"

"Before you finish, before you leave and don't come back, I want you to tell me why you're here."

Joe was about to let on with another half truth, but he could see that it wouldn't work. "Okay. Before were done, I'll tell you. I give you my word."

"For most of the people I've known in my life, that wouldn't mean much. But with you, I think that's as good as it can get."

Joe changed the subject. "Who are you most angry at, your mother and your father?"

"You mean 'was' don't you?"

"No. I mean who are you angry at?" Joe repeated

"They're dead Joe." Eric replied coldly.

"I know. But death doesn't stop how the living feel."

Eric crushed out the cigarette and studied the man. "That's true." He sighed. "My mother, I guess, if I had to say."

"Why?"

"She was…" He hesitated. "I thought she should of … ah, I mean, she wasn't what…" He shook his head. "I don't know." He rubbed his face with the accompanied clinking. "What was your mother like?"

Joe sat back and thought for a moment. "She was a very caring woman. Gentle and a little timid," he smiled, "She had a good heart and wanted what was best for everyone. She could get riled, but for the most part she was a soft spoken gentle lady."

"You had a good childhood I take it?"

"Yeah, for the most part."

"So it must be hard for you to relate to me?"

"Not really." Joe replied. "Years ago it would have been very hard for me to do so, but not so much now."

"And why is that?"

"It's just exactly what you said, 'Everyone has it in them'. When I was younger I didn't believe this but now I do. Absolutely."

Eric gave Joe a quizzical look. "In spite of what that Bible book says."

Joe grinned. "No, because of what that Bible book says."

"What do you mean?"

"You think you've done bad things, try this one on for size. A man makes a vow to God that if the Lord will hand over his enemies to him he will sacrifice the first thing he sees when he comes home."

"Yeah," Eric studied Joe closely.

"The first thing he saw was his daughter." Joe adds.

"So he backs out on his vow. People do it all the time, so what. I'm sure you've heard of foxhole promises."

"Oh, yes, I sure have. But this man, Jephthah, he didn't take his vow to God so lightly," Joe replied.

"Whatever."

"No. It's right there."

"He sacrificed his daughter for a stupid vow?"

"That's what he did." Joe confirmed. "How about someone who would kill thirty men because he lost a bet."

"Where's that in the Bible?" Eric questioned in doubt.

"Come on Eric, you've heard of Samson."

"Not that part of the story."

"Really. What about the two sisters that got their father drunk so that they could sleep with him?"

"What Bible do you read anyway?"

"The same one you used to," Joe answered.

"I never actually read it, but the stories that were told to me didn't have any of that in them."

"I don't suppose they would have. Not many people know that they're in there, not even your good church going folk."

"Why is it in there?" Eric was curious.

"Because it's the truth."

"It's pretty brutal truth for, 'the good book.'"

"Yep." Joe nodded. "I take it you didn't have any brothers or sisters?"

"Just me. That was probably enough, don't you think?"

****

Joe sat in his favorite chair and stared up at the painting of Washington on the wall with the book in his lap, and the only light coming from the lamp on the table next to the glass. He looked back down through his reading glasses at the words in the book and began reading where he had left off.

"For our struggle is not against flesh and blood, but against the rulers, against the authorities, against the powers of this dark world and against the spiritual forces of evil in the heavenly realms."

The voice of condemnation fell upon him like a wet blanket. "Now you're friends with the worthless piece of scum? Is that it? This vile man that deserves more than death. He should be tortured and made to suffer more than his victims did. Surely you don't think he deserves less than that!"

Joe looked up from the book and spoke out loud. "I would hate to reason on who deserves what?"

The voice in his inner ear dripped with dark sarcasm. "Oh, yeah. You're such a bad man. You know all about deserving punishment for doing wrong. You've killed so many people and committed so much adultery and stolen so many things throughout your life. Oh, wait, ha, ha, ha. You haven't done any of those things, Joe. You don't know what that man deserves because you have no idea the evil he has done. Are you now the judge and jury?"

The weight of the voice pressed down on him and clung to him like black tar. "Oh, Lord," he whispered.

But the voice of condemnation didn't leave. "Joe," it oozed. "Why do you put yourself out for such a vile excuse of a human being? Why do you waste your time?"

"Oh Lord," Joe whispered again, "help me." His breathing became labored as he struggled under the heavy spirit that oppressed him.

Condemnation spoke again. "It's useless. He's a lost soul with no desire for help. Stop wasting your time. It will do nothing but fill you with depression and anger if you keep going back. You won't be able to forget the things he tells you. They'll be burned into your mind forever. Already you see things you don't want to. It's useless, useless."

Joe set the book on the table and got down on his knees in front of the chair. "My God, please help me. Help me, oh Lord, my God, help me." He struggled to breathe as he pleaded. "Please, God, help me to do what you ask."

Then the voice of peace spoke soft and gentle. "Peace I give you. Don't be troubled."

Joe relaxed, took a deep breath and sighed. Exhausted he rested his head on the leather chair.

"It's all right." The voice of peace spoke once more in his inner ear. "It will be all right." Then a warm blanket of comfort wrapped around him. First his head and then down around his shoulders and then the rest of his body was enveloped in the cocoon of goodness. He smiled faintly as he rested against the chair.

"Why do I have to go?" He whispered to the voice of peace, but there was no answer.

****

That evening Joe went to his dad's house for dinner, Francine was also there. She busied herself setting the table and helping her grandpa prepare the meal for the three of them. Francine had moved back to town, willingly filling the gap left by her mother's death, doing her best to take care of both her dad and her grandfather.

"Where's those da-," Carl Ellison caught himself with a glance at his granddaughter, "-ang peas?" He grumbled as he looked around, making two turns in the middle of the kitchen.

"Grandpa!" Francine scolded him. "They're already on the table."

"Well, who put 'em there?" He scowled.

"You did," she replied calmly.

"Oh yeah, that's right." He picked up the baked ham and headed into the dining room, Francine right behind him with the glass pitcher of lemonade.

Joe came in from washing up just in time to see the delicious ham being set on the table. "Now that's a beautiful sight."

"Why thank you, Father," Francine responded playfully with a tilt of her head. "And the ham looks good too."

He smiled at his daughter's wit. "Yes, it does."

Her grandpa set the platter on the table, then gave it a once over. "Mm-mm. Perfect. All right, let's eat."

"I'm all for that," Joe smiled and took his seat at the end of table, opposite his dad.

"It all looks delicious," Francine added. They sat down and took each other's hand while her grandpa asked the blessing.

"Father, we thank you for the many blessings that you have given our family. We thank you for your guidance and for keeping us in your will. We thank you for providing for our every need. Thank you for the meal we are about to receive. In Jesus' name, amen."

"Amen," Joe and Francine repeated.

They began dishing up the food and passing it around. "So Dad," Joe scooped the sweet potatoes on his plate. "Mm-mm. I haven't had sweet potatoes in a long time."

"Yams." His dad responded immediately without looking up.

"Dad," Joe looked up, "they are sweet potatoes."

"Yams." His dad handed the plate of ham to Francine with a smile. "These are the same kind of yams your mother used to get, and I have never felt the need to change the recipe or the name."

Joe set the disputed dish next to Francine, who gave her dad a look that said to let it go. He frowned and picked up the dish of peas she had just set down. "How's Mr. Sumter doing these days?"

"Real good," his dad replied, "for an old fart that can't see or hear."

Joe smiled. "I thought we were talking about Mr. Sumter?"

"Very funny son. Your times coming."

Joe cut off a piece of ham. "How's work, honey?"

"It's going really well," Francine answered. "Jill, the girl I told you about…"

Joe nodded.

"Well, she's getting married."

"To whom?" Joe asked.

"To her boyfriend of course." Francine answered.

"Who's that?" Her father asked.

"Dad," she scowled. "I told you about him the other day when we were at dinner."

"I guess I was waiting to hear about your boyfriend."

"You got 'a boyfriend?" Her grandpa asked with enthusiasm.

"No." Francine replied.

"Then why'd you say she had a boyfriend?" He looked at Joe.

"I didn't." Joe answered.

"You just said you wanted to hear about her boyfriend."

"I did. And I would, if she had one." Joe looked over at Francine and winked. His dad sighed and shook his head.

"Pretty girl like her can afford to be picky." He smiled at her.

"Grandpa!"

"Just call like I see it," he answered.

"Now that I can agree with." Joe smiled and stuck a piece of ham in his mouth.

"Anyway," Francine continued. "Jill is so excited, and her fiance is a really nice guy. They're going to have a small, formal wedding. I think it's very sweet."

"Sounds wonderful," her dad replied. "I hope they have a very nice wedding day to start them on their way."

Her grandpa shook his fork to make a point. "A wedding is very important, even though most men would just as soon do without it. But it is significant to make that commitment public; it give substance to the whole event."

"I agree, Dad."

"Yes," Francine added, "I believe that is the type of wedding I would like to have someday."

"And so you shall." Her father replied.

She toyed with the food on her plate. "A friend of Jill's fiancée asked me to accompany him to the wedding."

"Really. Anyone we know?"

"I don't think so." She pushed the peas around. "He seems very nice."

"What's his name?" Grandpa asked.

"Adam." She finally filled the spoon with the pushed around peas. "Adam Randall."

"Randall, Randall?" Grandpa searched his mind. "Adrian Randall."

"No, Grandpa. It's Adam Randall."

"Oh, yes. I once knew an Adrian Randall. Fine fellow. Hmm. He died in Vietnam." Grandpa looked back to his plate. "Left a wife and son behind. Owned a garage down where they built that big store. I don't know how, or if, he ever made any money at it because he was always fixing people's cars even when they couldn't pay right away or at all. Good man."

"Well," Francine replied. "I don't if they're related. I've only known him for about three weeks."

"Three weeks?" Joe raised an eyebrow. "Really."

"I don't tell you everything." She raised an eyebrow back at him.

"Good." He replied. Like most dads, he really didn't want to know everything that his daughter did.

They all enjoyed their meal together with smiles and laughter, and after clearing the table they wandered into the living room for coffee. Francine brought a cup of coffee to her grandpa and went back for her own while Joe sat down with his.

His dad took a sip and then spoke up. "Are you still going down to the prison?"

"Yeah," Joe cradled his cup.

His dad shook his head. "I still don't understand it, I've tried,. I just don't see the purpose in it."

"Maybe there's nothing to understand," Joe replied. "All I know is, it's something I'm supposed to do."

"You always had a pretty good compass, but this time…well, I don't know." His dad took another sip. "Fella' like that needs to be shot in the head, not talked to."

"Well," Joe paused. "I can't say that I disagree with you. But, that's beside the point. Like I said, it's—"

"—just something you're supposed to do. I know." His dad finished the statement. "I still say he's a worthless ba—"

Francine came into the room, which cut his cursing short. "Okay. I think we can find more pleasant subjects to talk about." She sat down on the couch. "Something light and refreshing, you know, like politics or religion."

They all laughed and then spent the rest of the evening talking and laughing. Grandpa loved it when they came over and visited. It was always a special time for him.

The next morning while Joe was just fixing his first cup of coffee, the phone rang.

"Hello?" Joe answered.

"Hey Joe, it's Tom."

"Tom. What's up?"

"Do you really want to know more about Eric Chambers?"

"Yeah, I think so."

"You think so?"

"I think I need to know," Joe sighed.

"If you're up for a drive, I can take you to someone who knew him."

"Where?"

"It's about a two hour drive," Tom answered. "You good for it?"

"Sure. You want me to pick you up?"

"No, I'll swing by and get you. It's on the way."

After the long drive, Tom pulled into a Baptist church parking lot and then looked over at Joe. "This is it."

Joe looked up at the cross on the top of the steeple. "So, this minister knew Eric?"

"Yeah, fairly well form he said." Tom looked out the window. "You want me to wait out here?"

"No. You might as well come in, too," Joe answered. "Unless you don't want to?"

"I'd like to hear what he has to say, if you don't mind."

They were greeted politely by the church receptionist, a dark haired woman about forty.

"We have an appointment with Reverend Collins."

"Please wait here. Would you like some coffee or some water?"

"No, thank you," they replied at the same time.

She left them and went into the adjoining office. A few seconds later the minister came out, a tall thin man with a broad smile.

"Good morning, gentlemen." He reached out to shake their hands.

"Good morning." Joe was surprised by the man's firm handshake.

"Good morning" Tom answered. "I'm Tom Watkins; I talked to you on the phone."

"Yes, of course," the reverend nodded. Then he looked at Joe. "You must be Joe Ellison."

"Yes, call me Joe."

"Call me Brian, please, come into my office." He waved them ahead of him through the open door. "Hold all my calls until we're done."

"Okay," the receptionist replied with a solemn look. She appeared to know what the meeting was about.

Joe waited for Brian to take his seat before asking. "So, you knew Eric?"

"Yes I did." Brian nodded, looking Joe in the eye. "I knew him quite well; at least I thought I did."

"Do you mind telling me what you know?" Joe asked.

Brian looked hard at Joe. "Are you sure you want to hear it?"

Joe took a breath and then sighed. "I need to know."

He nodded. "A lot of people want to know what they're better off not knowing."

"That part I already know."

Brian sat back and began. "I don't know what he has told you, but I doubt it was the complete truth. He has a gift for deception, telling half truths and twisting facts just enough to make something seem different than it really is. He came here over twelve years ago. Walked in one day without notice. By that, I mean he didn't draw any attention to himself, just started attending our services and Bible study classes. I was impressed by his knowledge of the scriptures."

Joe gave Brian a quizzical look. "He knows the Bible?"

"Oh yeah, as well as anyone and more than most. He let on to the contrary?"

Joe nodded and then asked. "He wasn't a child when he attended your church?"

"No. Twenty-three, I think. And he knows the Bible from cover to cover, be sure of that. He was a polite, well mannered respectful young man. Got along with everyone real well. Started leading Bible studies and contributing to the church in many different ways. He, ah, he always had a distinct view of justice and was very passionate about the subject of judgment."

Brian paused and then continued with a little apprehension. "I can't prove what I'm about to tell you. No one could. But I believe he killed two of our church members. The Danburys. A married couple that was very involved in the church, very dedicated to the Lord. Some said they were a bit self-righteous and judgmental toward others. You see, they didn't have children, but were trying," the minister explained. "So when they would find fault with the parents of other church members, it didn't set real well. I have found that it's rather common for people to judge others in areas that they themselves either don't have a problem with or have not yet had experience on the subject. Like people that accuse drug addicts and alcoholics of being weak because they can't stop. But these same people that accuse them are gluttons, gossips and liars. Anyways, the Danburys did ruffle a few feathers with their assertion that true believers should be, and could be, perfect. They said it was just a matter of being self-controlled. I will admit that their legalistic point of view was a little extreme, but they didn't deserve what happened to them."

Joe and Tom sat silent and waited for the minister to continue. Hearing what was to come would be disturbing, at the very least.

Brian was looking down at the desk top, not eager to recall the event. "At first glance, the police thought it might be a murder-suicide, but they quickly saw that it was a double murder. Kevin, Mr. Danbury, had been tied to a chair with electrical cords while Pam, his wife, was tied on the bed. They had both been beaten severely and..." the minister cleared his throat, "Pam was repeatedly raped in front of her husband. The police psychologist said that whoever did it probably used them against each other: if she began to scream or make too much noise then Kevin would get beat, and if Kevin made too much noise, then Pam would get beat. From what they could gather, it had gone on all night long. Then Pam was strangled to death and Kevin was shot in the head. Probably in that order, they say." The minister looked sick.

Joe felt sick to his stomach and his dry throat made it hard to swallow. "How do you think it was Eric? Why wasn't he arrested and charged?"

Brian nodded his head in silence. "He wasn't arrested or charged because there wasn't any evidence linking him to the murders. As to why I think it was him, well, it was more what he didn't do that drew my attention. Even though Eric disagreed with Kevin, he would never argue with him. He didn't press his point on an issue, even though he did so with others. And the way he would look at Pam was not right. I could see it. Something was wrong, but I couldn't put my finger on it. I could feel it, though." The minister sat back and stated. "It's like a barking dog; they are loud and you know right where they are. They're not near as dangerous as the dog that doesn't bark. You know the kind, they slip up on you real quiet, with their eyes locked on you. The worst of them doesn't even growl, just attacks. Who and why they attack usually doesn't make any sense whatsoever."

Tom and Joe both nodded in agreement, but remained silent.

"That's Eric Chambers." Brian leaned forward. "When he was questioned about it, he had an alibi and was seemingly shocked and hurt by even being questioned. And when I pushed the issue, he didn't get mad or short with me or scared about the whole thing, no, he never mixed up his story or let on in any way. But one time, just one time he let it slip. Not with words, but in his eyes. Someone made the comment that whoever committed the murders was an evil genius. That's when I saw it, the look of pride. A puffed up ego is a hard thing to hide. It was just a spark, just a flicker in his eye that absorbed the compliment with glee. And he saw that I saw, but instead of getting nervous or panicking he simply returned my look with a cold dead stare. It was as if the dog was deciding to attack, or walk away. He walked away and I never saw him again."

Tom asked. "You told the police this?"

Brian nodded. "Oh yeah. But like I said, no evidence. Just a crazy preacher's gut feeling and a look. That's not enough to do anything. The police kept track of him for a while, but he came up clean on everything and they finally let it go. When I saw that he had been convicted, it confirmed what I already knew. But knowing didn't save anybody." He looked at the two men with anxiety and worry in his face. "What do you do in a situation like that? You know what he is and what he's done, but you have no proof. What do you do?"

Joe shook his head. "I don't know, I really don't know."

"You did all that you could," Tom added. "We can't arrest and condemn people on feelings, no matter how real and true they are. Even if the police believed you they would still need proof."

"I know," Brian replied. "But that doesn't make it better." He paused and then asked Joe. "You talk with him face to face, don't you?"

Joe nodded.

"You've felt it, haven't you?" The reverend squinted as he studied Joe. "The darkness, the coldness around him, you've felt it."

Joe nodded, but said nothing.

"It's not in him, but it's all around him." He studied Joe very closely and then said. "Your own battle is getting harder, isn't it?"

Joe didn't respond.

"It will get worse. Remember who the battle is against and who it is that overcomes. Your burden is great. You will be in my prayers."

Joe stood up, Tom and the reverend followed his lead. They shook hands and started for the door when Brian added. "Feel free to use any of the information that I have told you. If you think it would help, tell Eric I said hi, and that I'm praying for him."

This time Joe looked deep into the man's eyes to see if he really meant it. The reverend saw the question and answered.

"Not because I feel like, but because I need to, for my own sake."

"Thank you," Joe said before walking out with Tom.

The only sound was the thumping of the car across the bridge as the two men rode along in silence. It was almost two hours before Joe spoke up.

"When he asked what would we do in his situation, knowing someone is guilty but not having proof…"

Tom kept his eyes straight ahead. "Yeah?"

"Eric would kill them."

Tom shot a glance at Joe. "What?"

"Eric would kill them. If he knew they were guilty, he would."

Tom thought on it for a moment. "What would you do?"

Joe kept looking out the window as they left the thumping bridge. "In his situation, I don't know, maybe just exactly what he did."

"It's not very comforting." Tom said.

"What's that?" Joe asked.

"The fact that a sociopathic killer will carry out justice faster and swifter than law abiding citizens will."

"You're right, that's not a very comforting thought."

That night Joe sat in the same chair next to the table with the light and drink on it, the book in his lap and reading glasses on. He had read for an hour before his mind began to drift off and wander through the past days and the days ahead. He thought of his wife and mother, gone from this world and in a much better place. A place where there were no regrets of the past and no worries for the future. He smiled at the thought of being in eternal peace. He thought about his daughter and his father and how much he loved them. But his smile faded when all of a sudden he thought about Eric Chambers and the prison and the oppression he felt every time he went there.

He could hear his dad's voice loud and clear. 'Fella like that needs shot in the head, not talked to.' Joe rubbed his eye with the heel of his hand and sighed. He could hardly disagree with proposed solution.

Then he heard Brian's voice, 'I'm praying for him.' Yes, Joe thought, so am I.

Then he heard Tom, 'What would you do?'

"What would I do?" He whispered out loud.

Then that cold, unseen cloud began to settle down on his shoulders, and the voice of revenge began to whisper into his inner ear. "You'd want to kill him, just like he deserves. You know you want to. He's a dirt bag, scum of the earth. You heard what he did. Come on Joe; don't pretend you could care for someone like that. What would that say about how you feel for the people he killed? You'd be turning your back on them!

Joe whispered, "Pray for your enemies."

The dark voice laughed, low and haunting. "Yes, yes. How righteous you are. What a good man you are Joe." Then the voice quoted, "Anyone who looks at a woman lustfully has already committed adultery with her in his heart. Have you done that Joe? You've lied and stolen and gossiped and you've hated. So now you're going to pray for a condemned killer? Because your prayers matter? Your prayers carry so much weight that you think you can help the suffering and mistreated of this world?"

Joe's breathing became heavy as he struggled under the load that pushed down on him. "Oh Lord, help me."

"Help me, help me." The voice mocked him and then became deep and dark. "You pathetic worm. What kind of man are you? Who do you think you are! In the whole scheme of things, do you think you really matter? How arrogant! To think that you could change another person's life?

You'll screw it up, and you know it. Just like you screwed up your son's life!"

Joe was on his knees in front of the chair pleading. "Oh Lord, my

God, my Father in heaven, help me, oh my God, my Lord my God." He struggled to breathe, and gasped under the weight of the dark hand that pressed down upon him. "Jesus, Jesus, Jesus. Oh my Lord, my God." He pleaded again and again as he slid to the floor and lay prostrate face down in the room. "Oh my Lord my God, my God. Jesus, Jesus, Jesus." Joe struggled as if he was pushing against a great unmovable object. He couldn't move his arms or legs. "Jesus, Jesus, Jesus." Then the weight lifted from him and he lay motionless on the floor of his den, exhausted.

Joe heard a far away voice, a woman's voice, calling to him within his dream. No, not a dream, a nightmare. He saw them, in their bedroom, beaten and tortured. Crying, weeping, and begging for the other's life. Fear in their eyes, mixed with love. Their attacker had his back to him and then he turned around. It was Eric with a creepy, happy grin. Then Eric turned away and Joe called out for him to stop. The man turned around once more and Joe saw his own son standing there smiling! But who was the woman calling to him? He heard it clearer now. "Dad. Daddy?" Why was the woman on the bed calling him Daddy? Her face was bruised and blood trickled from her mouth she looked over at him. "Daddy?" Then her voice became louder and more forceful. "Daddy!"

He woke up with a start. Still lying face down on the floor, he saw someone's shoes. The person was shaking him awake. It was his daughter.

"Daddy!"

"Yeah." He breathed a sigh of relief to be free from the nightmare. "Yeah, I'm okay."

"Daddy." He face was full of worry and fear. "What happened? Why are you on the floor? You're soaking wet? What's wrong?"

"I'm all right." He closed his eyes and took a deep breath then he pushed himself up onto his knees. He was so tired.

"No, you're not all right. What's going on?"

He grabbed the arm of the chair and forced himself onto his feet. "It's okay, honey. Really."

Francine picked up his Bible and set it on the table with the full glass and lamp. "Daddy! It is not okay! It is not all right! Tell me what happened? Did you have a heart attack?"

"I wish," he mumbled.

"Oh, that's great," she sighed. "You're okay but a heart attack would be better than what you're currently going through. That makes sense."

"What time is it?" He asked.

"About eight."

"Hmm." He rubbed his face. "Let's make some coffee."

"Are you going to answer me?"

"After I get some coffee." He started off for the kitchen.

"Good Lord," she mumbled.

Joe started the coffee while Francine put cups on the table, along with cream and sugar, but she couldn't wait for the coffee to finish before she got some answers.

"Dad, you've been really stressed out and tired lately, how come?"

He didn't answer or turn around, but just kept staring at the coffee dripping into the glass pot. He searched for the words or an idea that could explain what he was going through. And he also debated how much he should tell her. "I've been having a few nightmares lately. Last night was pretty bad."

"It's because of those interviews you're doing at the prison, isn't it?" Francine had not said much about the subject but it was starting to bother her now. "It's getting to you. Why do you keep going back? It's tearing you up, I can see it."

He wished the coffee would hurry up. "It's not uncommon for preachers to feel extremely depressed on Mondays. Do you know why?"

"No."

"It's because they have preached a very good sermon on Sunday." His back was still to her. "But it's not only preachers; anyone who is doing the will of God will face persecution and doubt. They will come under attack because of what they are doing."

"Attack from whom?"

"From evil."

"Evil like demons and the devil?" She stared at her father who continued to watch the coffee drip.

"Yes."

Francine struggled with what her father was saying. She knew and believed what the Bible said, but all the stuff about demons and the devil took place during the time of Jesus, not in this day and age. Now a days that stuff was just in scary books and special effects in horror movies. It wasn't real. "Maybe it's just the nightmares?"

"That's part of it," he answered, "but it's more than that. I'm supposed to go back and talk to him, but I also want to know why he did what he did."

"So this is more than just an interview for a book?" She stated more than asked.

"Yes."

"Does this have something to do with Bobby?" she asked.

"I can't deny that has something to do with it."

"It won't bring him back. You know that," she said softly.

"Yes, I know. But I would just like to know why? I've always been that way, you know that." He pulled the pot from the burner and walked to the table. "I've always asked why things are the way they are or why people do what they do."

"Yes, but this is killing you."

"No. It's not killing me." He smiled and gently touched her hand as he poured the coffee in their cups.

"Have you looked in the mirror lately?"

"Look pretty bad, eh?"

"Dad, you look like you haven't slept in a week."

"Well, I feel better than I look."

"I've never known you to be a liar." She narrowed her eyes at him.

He smiled and sat down across from her. "I'm not lying. I have a peace about this whole thing. But when I start thinking I should stop, that's when I know for sure that I have to do it."

"Daddy…" She shook her head. "What do you want to get out of all this?"

"That's secondary," he replied. "The number one reason is because I'm supposed to go and witness to this man."

"He's a murderer?"

"Yes, he is."

"He's a horrible human being?"

"He's that too," he sipped his coffee.

"I don't understand." She shook her head.

"No offense, honey, but you don't need to. It's not your burden to bear, it's mine. And even though I don't understand it all, I understand enough." He paused for a second. "None of us are good, not really."

"But some people are worse than others."

"Are they? In the eyes of a perfect, holy and righteous God aren't we all found lacking? Don't we all fall short? It says that all wrongdoing is sin, and the least is as bad as the worst. Right?"

"Hmmm." She frowned at her father's knowledge and belief in the Bible. "I don't know. I just worry about you."

"Well thank you very much. I appreciate it, but don't worry too much."

****

Joe's footsteps echoed down the hall alongside the guards, as they approached the room, the dark gloomy feeling settled in and around him.

"You okay, Joe?" the guard asked.

"Sure Frank." He smiled. "I'm fine."

The big man gave him a questioning look. "All right, but if you need anything just holler."

"Will do, thanks."

A short time later, Eric was sitting across the table from him with a cigarette in his mouth and that same calm cool look on his face.

"Afternoon Joe." Eric blew smoke into the air.

"Good afternoon Eric," Joe replied. "I just returned from a trip."

"Good for you. Hope you had fun."

"Not much."

"That sucks," Eric answered. "If you're going to take a trip, you should at least have some fun."

Joe watched the face of the man across table very carefully. "Reverend Collins says hello."

The convict's eyes slowly lifted from looking at his cigarette until they settled onto Joe's and locked. The two men looked deep into the others mind as they searched for what they weren't saying. Eric saw that the man across the table knew the truth and Joe saw the spark that the Reverend had talked about. Eric stuck the smoke back in his mouth and took a long hard drag and then he blew it into the air once more.

"So what did the good reverend have to say?"

Joe hesitated before he answered. "He said he's praying for you."

"Ha." Eric laughed. "Is he now? Well that's real nice of him."

"You were never charged with that one," Joe said bluntly not wanting to play games.

"No." Eric replied. "Although I did hear that whoever did it was a genius."

"I believe the term was, evil genius." Joe came back.

Eric nodded. "Maybe that was it."

"Why would you do something like that?" Joe wasn't smiling.

"You're assuming quite a bit aren't you?"

"I don't think so."

"Hmm. You're free to think what you want."

"The reverend also says you know the Bible pretty well."

Eric grinned. "Well, I will admit I played a little dumb on that issue."

"How come?"

"Because it's all a bunch of bull s---." He flicked off an ash.

"Why do you say that?"

"It's a pretty good fairy tale, but it's nothing to hang your life on. It's full of sensational stories and impossibilities. Cowards and injustice are everywhere." He sat up in the chair.

"Jephthah killed his own daughter because he was afraid of God! I'd say he falls under the fool category, wouldn't you? And Samson? Murders thirty men because he loses a bet! And God was in this, remember reading that part?"

Joe nodded.

"And what about Abraham? Lies about his wife because he fears for his life. That shows a lot of faith, right? And then God tells him to murder his own son. Now this he can do! What a coward, lies to save his own life but is willing to murder his only son. And what kind of God asks a man to sacrifice his own child?" Eric sat back in the chair.

"So you think God is not just?"

"I'm saying that book is full of contradictions. When it says that God is love, and yet he's the same God that wiped out complete cities of men, women and children? If that's God then you can have him."

"You've murdered men and women for no reason at all and you call God unjust?"

Eric's left eye twitched as he glared at Joe. He took another drag on the cigarette and blew it out hard. "Never for no reason."

"You stalk and kill a woman? For what reason?" Joe pushed.

"Because I wanted to, and I could."

"So if God is the creator of everything, why can't he do what he wants to with it?"

Eric's eyes narrowed for a moment and then he responded, "I never claimed to be loving, did I?"

Joe changed the subject because he felt himself being drawn into a dead end. "What about all the people who believe what it says?"

"Hypocrites and fools. That's what they all are. Every damn one of those church going idiots is either a fool or a hypocrite." He took another drag and blew it out hard. "They preach what they cannot do themselves and the fools in the pew pay them for it. They go to church and follow all the rules because it's tradition. You have no idea how many times I heard someone say they went to church or paid their tithe or did what they did because 'that's what we've always done.' Hell, most of the people that go to church never even open up a Bible. They sit out there and believe whatever the man in the pulpit tells them." He swore bitterly.

"I thought you didn't curse?"

"Yeah, well, you thought I didn't know anything about the Bible either."

"Did you ever believe what it said?" Joe asked.

"No. I thought I did once, but no, I never really believed it." He crushed out his smoke. "I thought that somewhere, somehow that book held the secret to life and happiness, but it doesn't. The only thing real about it is the fact that evil exists, and this world is controlled by it."

"Why do say that the world is controlled by evil?"

Eric quoted. "According to the prince of the power of the air, the spirit that now worketh in the children of disobedience."

Joe replied. "And in regard to judgment, because the prince of this world now stands condemned."

"Condemned, but not convicted," Eric answered back. "Apparently he's alive and well."

Joe nodded. "I won't disagree with that."

"What are you doing here?" Eric snarled. "What are you getting out of all this s---?"

"I want to know why you did the things you did."

"So you can write a book about it?" Eric scoffed.

"No. That's not it at all." Joe sat forward in the chair. "I have to know how you can pass a life or death judgment on someone and why."

"I told you, because I can."

"There's more to it than that."

"How would you know?" Eric replied. "Besides, you're not telling me everything either. Nobody would come here and go through all this s--- just because they want to know why."

"Apparently people do a lot of things just because," Joe answered.

Eric grinned. "Apparently."

****

Joe was tired by the time he got home and staggered into the house. He poured a drink and sat down to try and watch some TV. He laughed at the thought that there was nothing to watch, despite so many channels. He usually went into the den to read, work, or study, but he would just as soon stay away from there tonight. He contemplated going to bed, but he knew he wouldn't be able to sleep, even as tired as he was. Maybe he didn't want to go to sleep for fear of what dreams might come. He was restless in his mind, body, and spirit. Exhausted, but restless.

He hated it, flipping through the channels hoping that he would find something that would take his mind off things. Maybe he should just get drunk and pass out, but he knew that wouldn't help. He did his best to just think of nothing.

And yet, he found out that trying to fill your head with thoughts of absolutely worthless things is not an easy task. Everything that he brought to mind would eventually bring him back around to the very things he was trying to not think about!

How could someone stalk and kill innocent people? Why would they do it? It seemed that these people had less trouble talking about how they did it than why. Even thought Eric had reasons for why he passed these judgments on others, it still left too many gaps. And more than that, what could he say that would make a difference in Eric's opinion of God? How could he ever convince someone that God is a God of love? Impossible!

Three a.m. and Joe was standing in a room with pictures covering the walls. The photographs were of girls, but not of a lot of different girls. There were about half a dozen and each one had their own space. They were beautiful young women with blondish to brown hair, medium height and thin. The photos were placed in a sequence starting from far away photos that moved closer with each shot until the dead, bloody body of the girl ended the collage.

But there was an obvious blank place on the wall, where a group of pictures was missing. Joe heard a noise and turned to see a man standing over a bed with a straight razor in his hand. Someone was lying in the bed, but he couldn't see who it was. All of a sudden, Tom was standing next to Joe with a picture in his hand from off the wall. He didn't show it to him. Instead he motioned for him to come over to the bed. Joe walked to the bed and saw that it was Eric Chambers standing beside the bed with a dead look on his face; he stared at Joe and then looked down at the bed.

Joe was afraid to look, he was afraid to see who was on the bed. Joe looked for Tom but he was gone. 'Tom?' He said as he looked around the room. 'Tom!' Then he heard Tom calling back. "Joe. Joe. Wake up. Joe!"

Joe woke up, startled to see Tom beside his chair in front of the TV. "Tom? What are you doing here?" Joe rubbed his face and sighed.

Tom straightened up beside the chair. "I'll make some coffee." He turned for the kitchen. "Go get cleaned up."

64

After a shower and shave, Joe came into the kitchen to the welcome smell of fresh brewed coffee. "That smells good."

"It is," Tom replied without smiling.

"What are you doing over here this early?" Joe acted like nothing was wrong as he went to the coffee pot.

"Francine called me yesterday. Said something about finding you passed out on the floor of your den. I can see she wasn't exaggerating."

"She's never been one to exaggerate." Joe poured his cup full and headed for the little table to sit down.

"Joe," Tom was serious. "I'm starting to question whether giving you that information was a good idea."

"Why would you say that?"

"It doesn't look like it's helping you."

"I'm all right." Joe sipped from his cup.

"You're a mess," Tom insisted. "It's obvious you're not getting enough sleep. Lord knows the last time you made yourself a real meal. The only time you eat right, is when someone cooks for you or takes you out. And unless I miss my guess you're being tormented by nightmares."

"You're a pretty good cop Tom." Joe smiled.

"This thing isn't going to push you over the edge is it?"

"No." Joe became a little more serious. "I know what's going on. I still know what's good and evil, and I still know why I'm doing it. I will admit it's not the most pleasant thing I've ever had to do, but that's really not the point of it."

"What do you think about him now?"

"He's a liar and thief of life. He has the ability to be extremely brutal and at times probably more animal than human, but he is definitely not insane."

"You've changed your opinion a little," Tom replied. "How come?"

"I think that maybe I was just hoping he wasn't that bad." Joe looked into his cup. "Maybe if he was insane it would be better, or if he was full of regret, or if he was confused. I don't know what I was hoping for, but the fact is he's a cold blooded murderer and I still don't know why. Or I just don't believe what he said."

"He is a liar," Tom offered. "What about the spiritual warfare you're going through?"

Joe studied his friends face. "You've been there before haven't you?"

"Oh yeah." Tom nodded. "It comes on you dark and heavy and from every direction. From friends and family and from within your very own self. Pulling at you with doubt, fear and anger. Am I close?"

"Pretty close." Joe nodded. "Did you find anything out about his mother?"

Tom sipped his coffee and set it down but didn't answer. Joe looked up at him and asked. "What did you find out?"

Tom hesitated. "I'm not sure I should tell you anything more about this."

"What did you find out?" Joe persisted, knowing his friend would tell him eventually.

"His mother died from alcoholic poisoning after she had been beaten bad enough to put her in the hospital. She wouldn't file charges on the guy and when she was released from the hospital she went home and drank herself to death. And that was that," Tom paused. "Almost."

"What do you mean almost?"

Tom got up and brought the coffee pot back over to fill the cups. "You know the woman he was convicted for murdering?"

"Yeah. Carol Mercer."

Tom put the pot back on the burner and sat back down, taking a sip from the hot cup. "She was the sister of the man that beat Eric's mom."

Joe nodded. "That makes sense."

"How so?" Tom was interested in Joe's opinion.

"He wouldn't go after the man because it would be to easily linked back to him so he goes after the closest thing to the man. Was the man's mother deceased?"

"Yes."

"And his sister was his closest relative?"

"Yes." Tom answered.

"He wanted to kill the man but he wouldn't take that chance so he made the man a victim of loss. He made him live with the vision of his sister being tortured and killed."

"You'd make a fair decent cop yourself," Tom complimented.

"Didn't Carol Mercer's roommate walk in on the whole thing?"

"Yep. She was supposed to be away on a weekend trip, but it was canceled because of snow. She came home on Saturday instead of Sunday. Walked right into the room with Carol Mercer tied to the bed and Eric standing over her. He plunged a knife into her chest and then went after the roommate. But the roommate didn't run or panic; she picked up a golf club and beat the crap out of him. She honestly tried to kill him but came up short on the effort. He spent a month in the hospital healing up from the beating." Tom took a sip and then went on. "We know that he has more victims out there, but we don't have any evidence that links him to any of the killings that fit the profile. We're pretty sure which ones are his because they're clean, as far as anything that would give the killer up, that is. He didn't keep trophies, or bring victims to his house, or leave any trace of what he did. He's different."

"You know the picture you gave me?" Joe changed the subject.

"Yes."

"Did it come out of a room with pictures, photos, on the wall?"

Tom gave his friend an odd look. "Yes."

"Some of the photos were missing?"

"Yes. How do you know that?"

"A person lying in a bed." Joe added.

"How do you know this?" Tom insisted. "Did you go there?"

"Kind of."

"Kind of?" Tom was troubled with this information. "No one was allowed in that room."

"I saw it." Joe looked down at his cup.

"How? When?"

"Last night. Or early this morning I guess."

"What are you talking about?" Tom was confused.

"I saw it in my dream. When you woke me up I was there. And you were there too." Joe looked up. "You handed me the picture. There were pictures of women on the walls on both sides of a bed. Except for a place where the pictures were missing on the left wall. The photos started out far away and then got closer and closer until they ended with the woman bloody and dead. Someone was in the bed, but I didn't look." Joe paused. "Eric was standing beside the bed with a razor in his hand."

Tom studied his friend for a long silent minute before he said a word. "If I didn't know better I'd say you were in that room. And I also think you're in a place that's not normal."

"I turned around to find you but you were gone. I called for you and that's when you woke me up." Joe took a sip from his cup.

"Do you realize what you're saying?"

Joe nodded but said nothing.

"There's no way to know this for sure," Tom said with some doubt.

"He described the scene to me."

"Well there you go. You're just remembering what he said and added some things to it. That's all."

"He told me about what he did, but he didn't describe the room."

Tom shook his head. "I don't know," he sighed. "Maybe you should talk to someone."

"Who?"

"I don't know? I sure don't know what to say."

"I'll be fine."

"Sure." Tom drained his cup and stood up. "I've gotta go to work."

"Thanks for stopping by. It'll make Francine feel better that you did."

"Only if I lie to her about how you're doing." Tom shook his head again.

"You don't need to lie." Joe remained seated.

"I'll call you later." Tom hesitated and then walked off. "Take it easy."

"Get out of here," Joe joked.

Tom waved without looking and left the house.

When Joe heard the door shut, he put his head in his hands and sighed, "Oh Lord." He was exhausted, so he got up and went to the bedroom and collapsed on the bed and fell to sleep immediately.

A dark, burdensome voice whispered into Joe's inner ear. "The cowardly, unbelieving, vile, and murderers, will be in the fiery lake of burning sulfur, they will not inherit the kingdom of God. They have sealed their fate for what they have done. You know that. You reap what you sow. Why do you worry for someone that has done what he has done? Why lose sleep over a man like that?"

He heard another voice whisper over the top of the first voice. It was calm and peaceful but strong. "All have sinned and fall short of the glory of God."

The first voice became low and graveled. "The wicked will not inherit the kingdom of God. Isn't that what it says?"

"None are righteous, not one," the second voice said quietly.

"Very rarely will anyone die for a righteous man, though for a good man someone might possibly dare to die," the dark voice argued. "He is neither good nor righteous!"

"But where sin increased, grace increased all the more." Then the quiet voice became a bright light that drove away all the darkness. It left Joe with a calm spirit.

3

Eric took a long hard drag on the cigarette and smiled at Joe as he let the smoke roll out of his mouth and nostrils. "You ready to tell me why you keep coming back here?"

Joe nodded and studied the convict across the table. He struggled to pull the words up. Part of him wanted to hate the man, but every time he went there he was pulled back by the words he had heard the night before and because he could see his own faults and sins all the more clearly. He couldn't love the man either, so it left him somewhere in the middle, between caring and not caring, between feeling sorry for him and feeling nothing. Finally he spoke up. "I'm here to offer you eternal life through Jesus Christ."

Eric laughed out loud. "Well, ain't you a saint." He took another drag on his smoke and blew it out. "Is this your good deeds earning you your own place in heaven?"

"No," Joe didn't smile.

"You're just feeling benevolent then. You're just a good man showing how good you really are, uh?"

"No. That's not it either."

"Then tell me, Joe. What would make a good righteous man like you come into this place and offer me salvation, as if you could?"

"Because, it's what the Lord told me to do."

"Oh, well now. We've got ourselves a prophet here. You talk to God, and he said for you to come in here and save me. Is that about right?"

"I can't save you, but he can. And yes he sent me in here to tell you that he wants to save your soul from eternal hell."

"You're full of --." Eric swore as he flicked an ash onto the floor. "I'm a confessed murderer, tried and convicted. I ain't here for shoplifting you know."

Joe was calm on the outside, but inside he was torn. He wanted to walk away, but something held him in his seat. "You're a sinner, and just like me you need a savior."

"What if I don't want a savior?"

"That's your choice," Joe answered. "I'm just here to make the offer. Take it or leave it. Repent and trust in Christ and find salvation, or don't and go to hell." It felt good to say that last part.

Eric stared at Joe with venom in his eyes. "Who the hell are you to come in here and act like God. Are you so righteous that God can only talk to you? Why doesn't he come down here and talk to me? Huh? You're not even a preacher or a priest. What gives you the right to tell me how to get saved?"

"Nothing," Joe answered frankly. "You're right. I'm not a minister or priest or preacher. I'm just a man that God told to go and do something, so I did it." Joe was getting angry. "Whether you believe it or not you can be saved from hell. But to tell you the truth I don't care if you do or not." Joe stood up and called for the guard. "Frank!" He turned back to Eric and looked him straight in the eye. "I don't give a s--- what you do. But you need to know that, beyond my understanding, God loves you and Christ died for you. Your salvation is based on whether you agree with God or not! And that's it! Nobody's good enough, not you, not me, not anyone! It is by grace and grace alone and not by any amount of good deeds! You're a despicable human being and God loves you! It's your choice, Eric! Admit you're a sinner in need of a savior and repent, or reject Christ and die in your sins and spend eternity in hell! I couldn't care less which one it is!"

Joe walked to the door where Frank, the guard, let him out and walked him down the hallway. Frank wanted to ask him about what he had just heard, but he could tell this wasn't the time or place.

Eric sat and stared at the door as the words that had been spoken to him tumbled around in his head. And long after they had put him back into his small cell the words would not leave him be. He knew the words in the Bible, but salvation had always been attached to being good, to doing good things and following rules and laws. But what the man had told him was something he had never heard. Or maybe he had heard it before? Maybe he just couldn't accept it?

No way. Joe was full of it! But why would he tell him this stuff? What purpose could he possibly have in coming all the way down here and lying to him? Impossible! After a whole life full of lies there was no way he could be saved now. This was about Joe feeling better about himself, doing a good deed to earn his own salvation. Notch up another soul saved on his Bible! But no matter how much he reasoned it all away, Eric could not sleep. The words would not leave his mind.

Joe felt horrible all the way home. His was sick to his stomach. The words he had yelled at Eric echoed through his mind. What had he done? How could he do that? He had failed, he had utterly failed. He had lost his temper and let the situation get the best of him. The Lord had sent him to present the gospel to another human being and he had failed!

Walking into the house he felt horrible. He went straight to the bathroom and tried to vomit, but all it did was cramp his stomach and bring tears to his eyes. He went to the kitchen and drank some water. He paced back and forth across the kitchen floor and drank another glass of water and then went into his den. He got down on his knees and began to pray and then started to cry. No words would come out of his mouth as he asked God to give him relief from his struggle and pain. He pleaded and begged for the pain inside of him to be taken away.

The dark accusing voice wrapped its clammy hand around him. He felt claustrophobic and it was getting hard to breathe. There was a burden, dark and heavy that pushed down upon him. "You failed. Everything you said drove him away. You failed at everything that you set out to do. You're worthless. What right do you have to tell anyone anything? You shouldn't be giving advice to people anyway."

"God almighty help me." Joe begged. "Help me, help me, help me. Dear Jesus, help me."

An hour later there was a knock at the door. It shook him out of his distant state of mind. The person at the door knocked again. Joe got to his feet and staggered to the door. When he opened it up, the Reverend Collins was standing there.

"Reverend?" Joe was surprised.

"Mr. Ellison."

"Come in, please," Joe stepped back and motioned for the man to come in.

"Thank you," the reverend looked uneasy.

"Would you like something to drink?" Joe offered.

"No thank you. I'm sorry to drop in like this. I tried to call but there was no answer. I called your friend Tom and he said you probably at the prison. I came over because, I ah, because…"

"Let's go into the den." Joe motioned. "We can sit and talk. Are you sure you don't want something? Water, coffee, tea?"

"I don't need anything, but it looks like you might."

"As a matter of fact I do. Do you mind if I make some coffee?"

"Not at all, and on second thought, I will take a cup if you're making some anyway."

Brian followed him into the kitchen, where Joe made a pot for the two of them. Joe turned to look at the man. "You've come a long way to tell me something."

The reverend looked down and sighed, then looked back up at Joe. "Okay, you're in a spiritual battle. You stand between hope and despair and you are being torn apart by doubt. God has chosen you to go to a man that not many would consider worthwhile to talk to, much less offer the gospel to."

Joe nodded but said nothing.

"You must be a man of great faith for the Lord to ask you to do such a thing, especially since, ah, since the extenuating circumstances."

"I don't know about that." Joe grinned. "I don't feel very faithful today."

"I know."

Joe furrowed his eyebrows at the man. "You do?"

"The Lord told me to come down here and encourage you. To tell you not to quit no matter how you feel. He has chosen you for this task because you can do it."

"I wonder." Joe took two cups from the cupboard. "Why not you? You knew him as well as anyone. You knew his victims. Why didn't you go on this errand?"

Brian dropped his head and remained silent for a moment before he looked back up. "I'm sorry to say my faith is lacking in this matter. Long ago I decided to forgive Eric and I pray for him and for me. But I'm afraid that my anger is still greater than my forgiveness. God help me. I wish I were strong enough to have been chosen for the task. But I don't think I could look him in the eye and sincerely offer him God's love and eternity. I don't think I could do it."

Joe chuckled at the irony. "Well, you should have seen me in action today. I don't think I offered God's love and eternity with sincerity and compassion. The fact is, I told him I couldn't care less what he did with the offer."

"But you did offer?" the reverend asked.

"Yes. In the poorest way possible, but yes," Joe shook his head. "I told him to take it or leave it."

"Good, good." Brian seemed relieved.

Joe poured the coffee and the two men went into the den. As they walked in the Reverend stopped just inside the room. He looked around and then said. "This is your prayer room."

"Yes."

Brian nodded. "You do battle in here. This is where you make your stand against the evil that opposes you."

"Yes."

"I feel it." He took a seat and sipped his coffee. "I was sent here to tell you, Joe Ellison, that those who are with you are more than those who are against you. There are angels watching over you and protecting you and you will not be pushed beyond what you can bear. You will overcome. Whether or not he accepts is not up to you. That is not where you succeed or fail. That's beyond you. That is between him and God. You are asked only to go and witness to him. You have to go back."

"I don't know." Joe looked up at the picture of Washington. "I really blew it today. I let my anger get the best of me. I told him, ah, I told him I didn't care what he did, or where he went."

"That's all right," Brian answered. "Really, he knows the message is from God and from you. Have you told him about, about...?"

Joe shook his head. "No, I haven't."

"Are you?"

"I don't know if I should. I gave my word that I would tell him why I was there, so I suppose I will."

"Yes, you should," the reverend nodded. "You will be pressed on every side by doubt and fear and you will be oppressed by unseen forces, but stay strong! Hold onto your faith; hold tight to the word of God! Remember you can save no one. It is the Lord who saves. It is he who rescues and delivers. You are the messenger, go and deliver the message."

"Why me?" Joe looked the man in the eyes. "Why was I chosen for this?"

"I don't know, but it is your cup to bear." The reverend paused and thought for a moment. "Maybe—maybe it's because you're the only one that can truly represent God's love to him."

The two men talked for another three hours before Brian left. But before he did, they got down on their knees and he prayed for Joe, and for Eric, and for himself.

After Brian left, Joe sat down in his chair in the den next to the table with the lamp on, a drink on the table and the book in his lap. He began reading and studying and searching. He lost track of all time—whether it was day or night, morning or evening. "Oh Lord, my God. Help me do this thing that you have asked me to do. I cannot do it on my own. My God! I don't want to do it! Help me oh Lord, my God. Give me wisdom and understanding. Give me strength."

The dark voice laughed in Joe's inner ear. "Why do you struggle about this? If anybody deserves death, it is this worthless human being. You're absolutely right to resist. Why should you of all people be asked to do this thing? Leave it alone, and let someone else go. If God really wants this thing done he'll send someone, or do you think you're so important that it can't be done without you? If God really is in control of everything then he can find someone to go. In fact, if he is all knowing and all seeing he already has someone on the way."

Then a still quiet voice gently spoke. "Whoever obeys my commands loves me. Do you love me?"

Joe whispered, "Yes, Lord."

"Do you trust me?" the gentle voice asked.

"Yes, Lord," Joe answered.

The dark voice slurred at him. "You couldn't even save your own son! Do you think you can save this convict? Will that make you feel better? Will that make up for your failure as a father? Will that earn you a place in heaven because of your benevolent attitude? Is this your good deed that will seal your position in eternity? Now it is your works that will save you?"

Joe whispered. "It is by grace through faith, not works."

The dark voice within him went on. "You know that everyone thinks you're being foolish. They think you're acting crazy. Common sense says you're way off the mark. People think you're losing it and maybe you are. Maybe you have imagined this whole thing. Maybe you really are crazy. You're hearing voices aren't you?"

Then the quiet voice responded, "Be still and know that I am God. In those days I will pour out my Spirit on all people and your sons and daughters will prophesy. My peace I give you. Take heart. Be strong and courageous. Do not be terrified or discouraged, for the Lord will be with you wherever you go"

A calm, warm, peaceful feeling fell upon Joe, and he basked in the glow of the light that enveloped him. Then the gentle voice spoke again, strong and firm, but with peaceful assurance, "Get up and go."

Joe wanted to stay right where he was within the warm glow of peace, but he forced himself to his feet and headed out the door when there was a knock at the door. When he opened the door, it was his dad.

"Hello, Son."

"Dad, what are you doing here?"

"Can we talk?"

"Sorry," Joe apologized. "I was just on my way out."

"You're going to the prison aren't you?"

"Yes."

"You can't do this," his father said sternly.

"Why's that?"

"You're going there to try and save him!"

"Not me, but God." Joe smiled, be it ever so slightly.

"He doesn't deserve that."

"Deserve what?" Joe questioned.

"To be saved!"

"If not him, then who?" Joe reasoned.

"Someone who hasn't committed the despicable things this monster has."

Joe paused and thought for a second. "What is sin?"

"What?"

"What is sin?" Joe shrugged.

"It's, ah, it's doing wrong."

"Wrong against whom?" Joe asked.

"Well, against your fellow man." His dad had settled down just a little.

"Then why does David say that he had sinned against God alone when he committed adultery and killed Uriah? Isn't sin rebellion against God?"

"I guess so."

"Doesn't the scripture say that all have sinned?"

"Yes."

"Doesn't it say that no one is righteous?"

"Yes. But after you're been saved that changes," his dad argued.

"Doesn't it say that anyone that knows the good he should do and doesn't do it sins?"

"I guess."

"And doesn't it say that if we claim to be without sin we deceive ourselves? And if we claim we have not sinned we make him out to be a liar?"

"But that's before we have been saved," his dad snapped back. "Once you confess then you don't go on sinning."

"So you're saying that you're perfect?" Joe questioned.

"No," his dad frowned. "It's just that I don't…"

"You don't sin?" Joe raised an eyebrow.

"That's not what I'm saying."

"Isn't it?" Joe asked, then went on. "But Dad, I'm not talking about someone who's saved. I'm talking about a lost soul that has never repented and confessed his sins. Can't that person be saved? Even in your legalistic world?"

His dad glared at him but couldn't reply.

Joe nodded. "You don't want him to be saved because of the pain he has caused so many people, because of what he's done. I know I have felt the same way." He paused, "but if we start talking about deserving, then we're all in trouble. If God's grace cannot save Eric Chambers, then who can it save? For if we are condemned by breaking the law, then we are all condemned and we have no hope. But if the grace of God can save him, who cannot be saved?"

Joe opened the door and looked back at his father.

"I am going to offer the gospel to a lost soul. If he repents and asks God to forgive him and accepts Christ as his savior, then he will be your brother in Christ and coheir to the Kingdom of Heaven. He will have passed from death to life. If he rejects the grace of God then he will die and suffer eternity in hell. Which will you pray for, Dad?" He turned to walked out, but something stopped him. He went into the den and picked up his Bible. He had never taken it before, but this time he was supposed to. He walked out and closed the door behind him, leaving his dad standing in the entry of his home.

****

The heavy cloud of oppression was not so heavy, not as oppressing, as the other times Joe walked down the hallway. He sat down in the grey-walled room and waited. He could hear the footsteps coming down the hall, closer and closer. Joe wasn't sure what to expect this time after what happened at the last meeting.

Eric came in, shuffling along in little steps as the chains clinked and jingled with every move. He smiled at Joe and sat down while Frank chained him to the chair. "Hello, Joe." He grinned.

"Hello, Eric." Joe waited for Frank to get done before he pushed the pack of smokes across the table.

"Thanks." Eric reached out and took the pack. "You brought something else today, I see." He pointed to the Bible that sat on the table.

Joe nodded but said nothing.

Eric hit the pack of smokes against his left hand, then opened it and shook a cigarette out, all without a word between them. He lit the smoke, took a long, hard drag, sat back in the chair, and blew a smoke ring. "You really believe that bull s--- you were telling me last time, don't you?"

Joe nodded. "Yes, I do Eric. With all my heart."

"So what you're saying is that anyone can be saved no matter what they've done. Is that right?"

"That's right."

"So what's the unpardonable sin?" Eric took another drag.

"It's the sin of dying without asking forgiveness." Joe answered. "The only unforgiven sin, is the one of not asking to be forgiven."

"It could be you need be locked up as much as me." Eric scoffed and took another drag. "So what about after a man's, ah, saved, what does he have to do then, huh?"

"You're either saved or you're not," Joe replied.

"Humph." Eric flicked the ash of his smoke. "So why are you here Joe, really? No bull this time."

Joe was silent for a long while before he spoke. "I had a son. He was not a good man at all."

"Like me huh?" Eric offered.

"Yes. Very much like you," Joe agreed. "He—he watched women too. He watched them and he killed them." He sighed. "I wanted to know why. Why would he do that? Why would he do the things he did?" He looked up at Eric. "Why?"

Eric nodded as he studied the man across the table. "It's hard to put into words, much less a word. But I guess it all comes down to power and desire. There's an overwhelming desire to do these things when the opportunity presents its self. The mind craves the feeling of the whole process: the stalking, watching, capturing and the look of fear in their eyes and, yes, the killing. It satisfies a hunger that is eating away at your insides, but only for a while. There's something about being able to cause so much fear in another human being that they'll do anything you want. It's addicting." He took a drag and blew the smoke into the air. "You said you 'had' a son? He's dead I take it."

"Yes." Joe answered.

"So, do you think that if you can save me you could have saved your son? Or, maybe, if you can't save me you could not have saved your son. That would take a load off your mind wouldn't it?"

Joe thought long and hard before speaking. "I must admit those very thoughts have crossed my mind, but that's not why I'm here. I'm here to tell you that God loves you. He loves you so much he sent his son to die for your sins so that you do not have to...if you repent and ask forgiveness and accept Christ as your savior."

"God loves me, eh. How do I know that? What proof can you give me of that?"

Joe hesitated and then spoke. "You and I have something in common."

"Your son." Eric said.

"My daughter," Joe slid the picture across the table. "The woman you were stalking for a year is my daughter. You missed this one when you cleared out the rest of the pictures. My friend on the force gave it to me."

Eric didn't move, but sat silent and stared at the photo.

80

"No one knows that it was you who was in that room. Only you and I," Joe went on. "I am in a hard place. You see, my son was a very sick man. And now I find myself looking at the man who saved my daughter...and killed my son."

Eric looked up from the photo and searched Joe's eyes to see if he was telling the truth. His doubt turned into amazement as he sat and stared at the man across the table. Finally he sat forward and spoke quietly, "Are you here for your son or your daughter?"

Joe never took his eyes off the convicted murder. "I'm here for you."

Eric's eyes narrowed as he tried to find a way to call the man a liar, but he couldn't. "I misjudged you," was all that he could say.

"It is not me. It is the Lord." Joe answered. "How can I hold anything against you for killing a wicked son, when it was my sins that killed a righteous son, God's son, and yet he forgave me? How can I not forgive you?"

Eric remained motionless and silent as Joe stood up, pushed his Bible across the table and put his hand on the photo. "All she knows is what her brother was, and that he was murdered. That is all." He picked up the picture and stood up. "Eternity rests in the balance of your choice. God loves you, Eric Chambers—with an everlasting love. There were two thieves, one on each side of Jesus. They both deserved what they were getting, they were both convicted criminals. One rejected the creator of the universe and the other said 'remember me.' That's all, just 'remember me when you come into your kingdom.' And that man was saved. He didn't perform any good deeds, he wasn't baptized, and he didn't pay any tithes or join a church. He simply believed in the Son of God for his salvation." Joe nodded. "You are on the cross Eric, but which cross are you on?"

Joe turned and walked to the door as Eric sat in silence and stared at the book in front of him. Why would this man come into this place to offer him this hope, especially after what he had done to him? He barely heard the footsteps as Joe walked down the hallway.

That night, in the small isolated cell, Eric Chambers wept. He had no memory of ever having cried in his whole life, but tonight he wept; with tears unending, he wept.

Joe's father was still at his house when he came home. He was sitting in the den, in the chair with the small table beside it and the lamp on it. He was staring at the picture of Washington on his knees in the snow beside his horse. Joe stood in the doorway of the den.

His dad spoke without taking his eyes off the picture. "I wonder? Did he pray for his enemies?"

Joe looked up at the picture. "I don't know."

"You're a better man than me son." His dad said.

"I don't think—"

"You were right," he cut Joe off. "There's no way around it." He looked around. "Did he listen?"

"Yes," Joe nodded. "He listened."

"Did he…?"

"I don't know," Joe shrugged. "But I'm done. And I—I'm not supposed to go back."

"You left your Bible?"

"Yeah."

"You've had that for a long time. Isn't it the one your mom and I gave you?"

"Yes it is." Joe shook his head. "It's all marked up with highlights and notes. The pages are worn and tattered with stains on them. I guess I should have given him a new one, but I was supposed to give him mine. I don't know why."

"You remember that pocket knife your grandpa gave you?"

Joe smiled. "Yep. Worn pretty thin."

"One look at that knife told you a lot about the man that carried it."

"Yea. Told you he used it, regular."

"Yep. He carried it everywhere, used it all the time. Trusted it. That's what he'll see when he opens that Bible."

Joe looked at his dad and smiled.

****

Joe sat in the room with the other witnesses and watched as Eric was strapped into the chair. The convicted murderer looked over toward the witness room, but remained calm and quiet. With no resistance he was given the injection and died.

When Joe was leaving, Frank came up to him. "Joe."

"Yeah?"

"Here," he held out Joe's well worn Bible. "This is yours."

Joe nodded and took the book from the solemn guard. "Thanks."

"Um. I—I mean, you know that I heard most of what you said to him."

"Yeah."

"I—I have some questions if I could talk to you some time?"

"Sure," Joe replied. "We can do that."

"I was talking to a couple other guys who have a few questions of their own and they'd like to come along."

"We can do that."

"Great," Frank grinned. "I appreciate it."

"No problem. Just give me a call and we'll set up a time."

"Thank you." Frank took hold of Joe's hand with a firm grip. "Thank you."

When Joe got home he went into the den and sat in his chair. He opened the book and for some reason he turned to the back, where he saw someone else's writing. It must be Eric's. It said,

You have shown me how much God loves.

The phone rang.

"Hello…Yes. This is he…Yes, I knew Mr. Chambers…What is it he wanted?... Yes. I will pay for that…Thank you."

****

Joe stood at the grave site and looked down at the headstone that marked the place where Eric Chambers had been laid to rest. He smiled at the engraving.

There is no one righteous,
not even one.
SAVED BY GRACE